MW00940567

TITLES BY NADIA LEE

THE BILLIONAIRE'S FORGOTTEN FIANCEE
THE BILLIONAIRE'S SECRET WIFE
THE BILLIONAIRE'S HOLIDAY OBSESSION
MERRY IN LOVE
THE BILLIONAIRE'S COUNTERFEIT GIRLFRIEND
MERRY IN LOVE
FOREVER IN LOVE
SWEET IN LOVE
REDEMPTION IN LOVE
REUNITED IN LOVE
VENGEFUL IN LOVE

The Billionaire's Secret Wife

The Pryce Family Book Three

nadia lee

For James.

PROLOGUE

Ten years ago

JUSTIN STERLING WRAPPED HIS ARMS AROUND the soft, slim body of Vanessa Pryce, relaxing in the afterglow. The top-floor hotel suite was dark, mirroring the desert blackness that floated beyond Vegas's garish lights. The AC was putting out cool air, and now that the lovemaking was finished, she shivered. He pulled a sheet over the two of them.

They'd been dating for almost five years. Justin had attended Stanford for his Masters in order to be close to Vanessa, even though his great-uncle had thought Harvard Business School would be a better option. Nobody knew they were seeing each other, though. She wanted to keep things low-key to avoid drawing attention to their relationship.

Justin didn't mind if it made her feel better. Also, he knew his status as the Heir Apparent to one of the richest and most influential men in the world could destroy the privacy Vanessa wanted. There was a reason she tried to keep a low profile despite her own family's considerable wealth and prestige, and she avoided talking about them as much as she could.

She pressed her cheek against his chest. "You know I'm going to start my job soon," she said quietly.

"L.A., right?"

"Mmm-hmm."

He pushed his hand gently through her silky hair. She always dyed it apple red, even though her natural black looked stunning. She took after her mother, who'd been a renowned beauty in her youth. "We can probably accommodate each other's schedules. Now that I have my MBA, I need to be in Chicago for awhile, but it's not that far."

"Justin…" She cleared her throat. "It's probably better if we break up."

His hand stilled. "What?"

She sighed softly. "Long distance relationships never work."

"You don't know that."

"I think I do. We'll both be busy with our careers, and you're going to be surrounded by beautiful women in Chicago. You'll want to date them."

"Ohh, the women in Chicago. *They're* the problem. I guess all the handsome actors in L.A. won't be a factor." Justin said, keeping his tone light, even though the idea sent a fiery jealousy blazing through his body.

She laughed softly. "No, I'm not really interested. Besides, most of them want to date people who can help their careers, and lawyers don't really count. Not enough studio connections."

"Not if the lawyer's worth fifty million bucks."

She pressed her mouth against his. "Justin. Stop arguing. We still have until morning."

"Oh. So our breakup starts in the morning?"

"Yup. Let's not waste the night."

When she fitted her body to him, Justin let his annoyance go. She'd change her mind.

Except she hadn't.

November, one year ago

Ten years of on-and-off dating. No, you couldn't really call it dating. The more accurate term would be booty-calling. A week's conference in New York, a business trip to San Francisco, a secretly planned mini-vacation in the Bahamas. Two or three times a year, sometimes more, they'd find an excuse—or make one—to get together. Even though Vanessa's prediction about their careers seemed to be playing out, they couldn't really let each other go.

He stewed over that as he'd walked along the night streets of downtown L.A. after leaving his friend—and Vanessa's brother—Iain at a club. Vanessa had been so odd when he'd shown up at her firm, all uptight and aloof. Nobody, not even Iain, seemed to know what was wrong with her.

Instead of trying to figure out Vanessa's inexplicable mood, he needed to leave for Houston. His great-uncle Barron would kill him if he didn't show for Thanksgiving, especially since it was the first one he was celebrating with his girlfriend and her family…who also happened to be their in-laws now.

Then he heard the laugh that never failed to grab his attention. Throaty and full-bodied, it flowed over him, warming him from the inside out. He turned his head, and there she was.

Carrying a briefcase and a purse, Vanessa was striding along confidently in those crazy sexy stilettos of hers. Her red hair glinted as she tilted her head to look up at a man next to her.

Justin narrowed his eyes. The other guy was a bit too close to her for Justin's taste. He undoubtedly wanted to sleep with her. Given the man's conservative haircut and outfit, he was probably a lawyer. Maybe another associate at the firm where she worked.

Suddenly Vanessa stopped as though she'd felt something, then turned and saw Justin. Her eyes flickered for a moment, then a blank expression descended upon her face like she was looking at a stranger.

The persona-non-grata treatment scraped his already shot nerves. He could still hear her moans, smell the sweat and sex on her skin when she'd come with his cock buried deep inside her the last time they'd met for a hook-up. The memory of her sweet, baked-pear scent sizzled through him like a potent drug, and she was standing so close to the other guy that Justin knew her date could smell her.

The man next to her smiled at Justin. "Hello, Mr. Sterling. Fancy running into you here."

Justin gave him a warm, professional smile, while imagining breaking his nose. "Have we met?"

"No." The other man flushed. "But I saw you at the firm. I'm Felix Peck. An associate."

"Nice to meet you, Mr. Peck."

"Please. Call me Felix."

Justin nodded once.

Felix cleared his throat, shifting his weight. Vanessa put a hand on his sleeve. "If we don't hurry, we're going to be late."

Justin reined in his temper. "Do you mind if I borrow Vanessa for a moment, Felix?"

"Sure."

Justin pulled her away, none too gently, breaking the offending contact between her and Felix. She glared at him, but he didn't give a damn right now. If they'd been in private, he might have done something far more glare-worthy than just moving her a few feet.

When they had a little distance from the associate, she hissed, "Stop. What's wrong with you?"

"What's wrong with me?" Justin almost snarled at her. "Don't you know?"

"No. I can't read your mind." She yanked at her arm, but he didn't let go.

"It hasn't even been a month since you and I were fucking like bunnies, and you're clinging to this guy Peck? Do you think he can give you what I gave you?"

Even in the dark, Justin could see her cheeks flush. "Don't be nasty and weird. And hypocritical. It's not like you've lived like a monk since then. I've seen more than one picture of you with a model on your arm."

"Only because you didn't want to go to any of those functions with me."

"Justin…" She squeezed her eyes shut in frustration. "I like you, but it's complicated."

It suddenly hit him. The clarity of the situation—this messed up relationship he had with Vanessa—it was so obvious.

She was his Siren—the seductive, irresistible being that would lead him to his doom. Because no matter how much he wanted her, he couldn't really have her. And what she did to him wasn't healthy.

By indulging her, he was letting her screw with his mind.

He slowly let go. "I understand how it is now."

"Good," she said, rubbing her arm. "Now if I can—"

"I've let you use me for far too long."

She pulled up short. "Huh?"

"Because I liked you." He swallowed a bitterness that threatened to suffocate him. "Good enough to fuck in private, but not good enough to be seen with in public? I get the message loud and clear."

"What? No, that's not it." She took a step forward, her arm extending. "Justin—"

He pulled away, making sure they didn't touch again. "Don't even try. And don't ever act like you know me." The finality of what he was about to say burned his throat. "From now on, you're dead to me."

Then he spun and stalked away, blocking out Vanessa's cry. He'd had enough of this emotional rollercoaster bullshit.

ONE

Present day

VANESSA LET OUT A LONG BREATH AS SHE and Felix walked out of the firm's glitzy lobby to grab a latte from Starbucks. Her head throbbed, but she clenched her hands to avoid rubbing her temples. The client was guilty as hell, that was obvious, but she and other lawyers at the firm would spend endless billable hours to ensure a *Desirable Outcome*.

"You okay?" Felix lowered his voice. "You seemed really distracted in there."

"I'm okay." But she wasn't. Her oldest brother Dane had texted her in the middle of the deposition: *Parents are divorcing*. And now the jerk wouldn't answer her calls or texts.

"Miss Pryce!"

Vanessa stopped as two young girls ran toward her. Just like that the throbbing in her head started to dissipate, and she felt her mouth start to curl into a smile. They were clients from a previous case on which she'd worked pro bono. She turned to Felix. "Do you mind getting me a tall skinny latte? I'll meet you back upstairs."

He nodded and walked away, leaving her alone with the girls. "What are you two doing here?" she asked. "Does your dad know?"

The younger girl nodded. "Dad drove us. He was coming to downtown anyway." She hugged Vanessa's legs, her small hands sticky. "Dad's so awesome."

The older one, Suzy, added, "We wanted to see you and say thank you again."

Vanessa grinned. She'd fought long and hard to get their no-good drug addict mom and her abusive boyfriend away from the kids. It hadn't been easy to convince the court that the girls were better off with their father. The man was a gruff, blue-collar high school grad, while their mother had gone to community college and knew how to work the system.

"Aunt Sally said you didn't get paid. Is that true? I brought some money." The younger one reached into her pocket and pulled out a small change purse.

Vanessa put a hand over the girl's. "I've already been paid, just to see you guys this happy."

Their father rushed over and gathered the kids around him. "I'm so sorry they're bothering you. I told them they weren't going to be able to see you again, but they just wouldn't listen," he spoke fast, his face flushed.

"It's all right. I was on a coffee break. It's great to see them doing well." When she'd first met them, they'd been skinny, dirty and wary. Now they clung to him, their gazes certain of his love.

He sniffed. "Couldn't have done it without your help. *Thank you.*"

"I'm just glad everything worked out."

"I don't want to take up too much of your time. I know you're a busy woman, helping people like me." He turned to his daughters. "Hey, say thank you to Miss Pryce, real polite now, and then we can go have ice cream."

The girls crowed, their faces flushed, then thanked her again in a loud chorus. Chuckling, the man started herding them across the street. Something warm and sweet unfurled inside Vanessa as she watched them laughing and joking around. She blinked away sudden moisture in her eyes. *Now that*, she thought, *was a Just and Proper Outcome.*

It sort of sucked that her paying clients rarely fit into the same category.

She started to turn away, then stopped when she saw her mother climbing out of her car. She was dressed as elegantly as usual. Nothing about her hinted that something as disastrous as divorce was about to impact her life.

"Mom!" Vanessa started marching toward her mother at a rapid pace.

Ceinlys's face relaxed into a smile. "Hello, dear," she said when Vanessa was close enough to hug.

Vanessa searched her mother's expression, looking for any signs of distress, but Ceinlys looked perfectly composed. Still, Dane wouldn't have sent a text like that for no reason. "Is it true?" She'd kill him if he'd only done it to make her ask stupid questions.

"Is what true, dear?"

"That you and Dad are divorcing." It couldn't really be happening. Both her parents were in their *sixties*. Why now?

Ceinlys hesitated for half a second, then said, "Yes."

The answer hit Vanessa like a hammer to the base of her skull.

"Where did you hear that?" Ceinlys asked.

"Dane told me." Bitterness bubbled. "Why is Dad doing this?"

A wry smile twisted her mother's mouth. "You have it wrong, dear. *I* am divorcing *him*."

This time it was like a sledgehammer. "Why? The prenup—"

"If you wish to talk about my divorce, call my lawyer." Ceinlys's diction was proper and precise.

"Her name is Samantha Jones, and as it happens I'm late for our appointment."

Something cold and hard fisted around Vanessa's chest. Samantha was one of the most well-known divorce attorneys in California. Nobody hired her unless they were serious, and she was exactly the kind of lawyer her mother needed if she wanted to leave her father. Vanessa forcibly drew air into her tight lungs. "But—"

"Don't you have to go back to the office? It's only four thirty."

As if to prove her mother's point, Vanessa's cell phone started ringing.

"Nice chatting with you, dear." Ceinlys walked away. She didn't look back.

HANDS STEEPLED TOGETHER, JUSTIN WATCHED THE man on the other side of the executive desk. In his mid-forties, he looked starkly white against the dark, supple leather of his seat. His fish-like mouth moved, and words kept pouring out in an unrelenting stream, but Justin had tuned him out. It was too late for excuses.

"Have you heard anything I said?" the man said finally.

"Unfortunately, I have. Nothing you said can

change my mind. The children's hospital is no longer under your directive."

"But—"

The muscles in Justin's jaw tightened. This was getting tiresome. "Furthermore, as of now, you are no longer employed at Sterling & Wilson."

The construction manager's eyes bulged. "What? You can't do that!"

Justin gave him a bland look. "I just did."

"But Barron—"

"Is no longer in charge." Justin put some steel behind his voice. People kept looking for Barron even though he hadn't been in the office in months. It was getting old. "He's retired."

Sweat beaded on the other man's forehead. "Look. I know I made a few mistakes. He wouldn't like you firing one of his longest-term managers over some minor errors."

"Your 'minor errors' are going to cost the company at least five million dollars. You're not worth anywhere near that much money."

"I've managed hundreds of projects!"

"With an acceptable level of competence, for which you were compensated accordingly. But frankly, you aren't as good as you think you are. If you don't walk out of here in the next three minutes, I'll have you thrown out. The choice is up to you."

With that he dismissed the manager from his

thoughts as he focused on the papers in front of him. The Ethel Sterling Children's Hospital had been Barron's pet project, something he wanted to build in his late wife's name. It should've been completed two years earlier, but somehow it was still on-going. Barron hadn't really given it the attention it required, what with the return of his granddaughter Kerri from self-imposed exile and her wedding, plus Barron's own newly minted romance. And Justin had had other things demanding his attention since he'd taken over as well.

Justin glanced at the desktop clock. The round face was set in an elegant miniature silver statue featuring two swans with necks entwined. Their diamond eyes sparkled. Vanessa's eyes had sparkled the same way when she'd given it to him as a birthday present six years ago. They'd been in Paris on a secret vacation. He'd even booked separate hotel rooms to maintain the ridiculous façade she'd wanted.

He kept thinking he should throw it out, especially after their nasty fight in November, but somehow in the ensuing three months he hadn't been able to do so. He told himself the clock was useful, and it was true that it was the only timepiece in his office.

Almost six o'clock. He should have his assistant order him something quick to eat. It was going to be a long night.

His personal mobile rang, and he scowled at it. Fewer than twenty people had the number, and the last thing he needed was another problem. A frown creased his brow when *Iain Pryce* flashed on the screen. He was one of Justin's closest friends and Vanessa's older brother.

What could he want?

"Hi, Ia—"

"*Thank god.* Are you in Chicago?"

"Yeah. What's up?"

"It's Vanessa."

Justin's mood instantly darkened, then turned to something that felt suspiciously like worry. He cursed himself and kept his voice even. "What about her?"

"She's on a flight to O'Hare."

Justin pressed a finger against the spot between his eyebrows as his idiot heart thumped. She couldn't possibly be coming to visit him. "On business?"

"No. Can you get her off the plane and keep her there until I can go get her?"

"Isn't she flying private? Just have the pilot turn back to L.A." Unlike three of her brothers, she didn't have her own jet. She was probably on one of her brothers' toys.

"She's on United." Iain rattled off the flight number and arrival info.

I should just say no. He wasn't Vanessa's keeper,

and he really needed to forget her and move on. On the other hand, what was making her to come to Chicago? The moronic part of him spun a ridiculous fantasy: maybe she was coming to apologize and change her ways. Toxic hope. He didn't buy it.

"Justin, can I count on you?" Iain was saying. "I'll be there soon."

"Don't bother. It's late, and I'm sure you have better things to do," Justin said. "I'll send her back to L.A. as soon as possible. If not, I'll call. Is that cool?"

"Thanks. I owe you one."

Justin hung up and leaned back in his seat. *Yeah. You and everyone else.*

VANESSA RUBBED HER TEMPLES AS TWIN HAMMERS pounded inside her head. Maybe she shouldn't have had so much to drink on the flight, but this was a special situation. The cabin started to hum with activities as soon as the plane reached the gate.

The purser's calm voice came through the PA system, saying the usual about thanking the passengers *blah blah blah*. Then there was something different. "Please resume your seats for a few moments until we're cleared to deplane."

There was a general murmuring, but the passengers slowly sat back down. Vanessa frowned, taking her seat again with her purse clutched in her lap. She wanted to get off as soon as possible and then…what? She closed her eyes. Coming to Chicago was a mistake. She and Justin didn't have the kind of relationship where she could just show up unannounced for support. She'd systematically discouraged him from starting the type of deep conversation that she wanted right now. Her fingers tightened around her purse.

There's probably another flight leaving for L.A. soon. O'Hare was a huge airport. If not, she'd just check into a hotel and catch the first flight out.

A few moments later, the cabin door swung open and three men in uniform entered. TSA or ICE, she thought, her tired eyes bleary and unable to focus. She should sleep and eat better, but she hadn't been able to do either since November.

They came down the aisle and stopped at her seat. "Vanessa Pryce?" one of them asked.

"Yes?"

"Would you mind coming with us?"

That had an instantly sobering effect. "What's this about?"

"We can't say."

She narrowed her eyes. "Won't say" would be more precise. The men's expressions showed zero emotion, nothing she could use to figure out what was going on.

"Can I bring my purse and laptop bag?" she asked.

"Yes, of course." They stepped back.

She pulled out her bag, her mouth set in a tight line. Curious stares from other passengers burned her like a brand, and she suppressed a sigh. The one time she flew on impulse, and this was what happened. She pushed down her irritation and embarrassment. It was probably a mix-up. They were probably looking for another Vanessa Pryce, one who was probably some sort of dangerous fugitive.

The men escorted her all the way through the concourse. Many people didn't even pretend to look away. Why should they? It wasn't every day you got to watch a woman get dragged away by a team of uniformed government men.

"Do I get a phone call?" she asked finally.

"You can call whoever you like."

There was no one else to call except Rosenbaum, McCraken, Wagner and Associates. They were her family's lawyers, and they'd know what to do. She didn't feel comfortable representing herself, especially not while she was drunk and tired.

They led her to the other side of the security line. She was getting her phone out when they said, "Have a nice evening."

She turned back toward them. "Wait. Aren't I under arrest?"

One of them cracked a small smile. "What gave you that idea?"

She raised both of her eyebrows. They had to be

kidding. All that humiliating display for this? "Can I have your names?" She'd sic the family lawyers on them.

"Vanessa."

She stilled at the familiar voice, then turned, the three men forgotten. Justin watched her, his eyes hooded. A long black coat covered his lean body, and his mouth was set in a tight line, not a hint of softness or welcome in his expression. It made her feel small and uncertain. Why had she thought it would be such a great idea to fly out to Chicago? It would've been better if she'd stayed in L.A. and gotten drunk with her friends instead.

Except she didn't want to talk about her parents with anybody in L.A.

"What are you doing here?" Vanessa asked. "You aren't..." She stopped, taking a quick glance around the arrival lounge. No one in Justin's family flew commercial. The Sterlings had more money than they could spend in ten lifetimes.

"I'm here to pick you up."

Then it hit her; he was the one who'd sent those men. She waited for anger to surge, but instead resignation pooled in her belly. He'd made it clear how furious he was with her. "You're dead to me" was pretty final.

Now his gaze was raking over her. "If you were going to come to Chicago, you could've at least dressed for the weather."

"Oh." She looked down at her dark navy skirt suit and open-toe stilettos, perfect for February in L.A.

"Do you have anything warm in your luggage?"

She shook her head. "I didn't really, you know. Pack."

The muscles in his jaw bunched, but he came over and draped his own coat around her. It was toasty and smelled of winter and chocolate and Justin. In his Italian suit, Justin's shoulders looked so wide and comforting. Before she could get a hold of herself, tears sprang to her eyes, and she blurted, "My parents are divorcing."

Something shifted in his expression, and she could swear she'd glimpsed a hint of softness underneath the hard mask. And it only made her want to cry harder because he'd been such an amazing friend and support to her, and she'd pushed him away.

"I'm sorry." She wiped the tears. "I shouldn't have come."

There was a long, agonizing moment, and she wondered which way it was going to go. "No, it's okay," he finally said. "We can talk in my car."

"Where are we goi—?"

"Where else? To my place."

TWO

IT DIDN'T TAKE MUCH TIME FOR THEM TO REACH his penthouse. Justin's driver maneuvered the black Bentley through the wintry streets of Chicago, while Justin settled next to her. She started to raise her hand to reach for him, then stopped. He sat with his back unnaturally straight and stiff, his eyes contemplating the glittering city. His usually neat, dark hair was mussed like he'd just rolled out of bed, and it brought back memories of their times together.

Vanessa looked down at her expertly manicured hands. She still didn't know why she'd gotten on that flight to O'Hare. She and Justin had ended things. No…he'd ended it because he'd been furious with her. She'd never seen him so angry before, and she knew she'd ceased to be a part of his life since November.

And yet here they were.

When the elevator door opened on the top floor, Vanessa peeked at the place she'd made sure never to visit. She'd also ensured he never came over to her places either. They'd done everything at hotels, resorts…once or twice out in nature on camping trips. It wasn't that difficult to arrange a clandestine hook-up. After all, she'd learned from watching the best—her parents.

Justin's home was surprisingly inviting, with comfortable-looking couches and earth-toned furniture in sharp green and silver accents. Given how immaculate everything was—not even a speck of dust—he probably had housekeeping.

Justin brought her inside and gestured at a seat. As soon as she took it, he poured himself a finger of whiskey from his bar and downed it in one near-violent tilt of his head.

"Have you eaten?" he asked.

"No," she said, surprised at the realization that she hadn't had anything to eat since breakfast.

"No wonder you look so pale. Chinese or pizza?"

"I'm not hungry, but I can use some liquor if you have any."

"You're not touching a drop of alcohol until you have some food."

The hardness of his tone penetrated her misery and confusion. He was still furious with her. Why was he doing this then? "Justin, I don't… This was a bad idea. I'll check into a hotel." She got up and blinked as dots swam in her vision.

Cursing, he caught her. "Sit down and don't even think about it." He dialed a number and ordered two dinner specials.

She covered her face in her hands and breathed in Justin's scent on the coat. It was still around her, its presence comforting. She should take it off—it was quite warm in Justin's penthouse, but she loathed to give it up. Why was she even there? She knew how bad this thing with Justin was. When he'd finally ended it, made it clear how much he hated her, she should've left it at that.

"If you eat, I'll let you have a Mouton '45," Justin said finally. The couch dipped under his weight.

"Thanks," she said without looking at him. She must look awful for him to offer one of his prized Moutons.

"So. Is it really true? Your parents are divorcing?"

She nodded. "Dane told me."

Justin let out a long sigh. "All the brothers you have, and it had to be him."

Her mouth twisted. "I thought he might have been kidding, but when I spoke with Mom, she told me she'd hired Samantha Jones." Vanessa clenched her hands and blinked away tears. "And if that wasn't bad enough, Dad said it wasn't up for discussion." *Doesn't concern you, Vanessa. You aren't my attorney.*

No. She was just their daughter. Two of her brothers—Iain and Mark—had been confused about the news, Dane as usual had nothing illuminating to add, and Shane…she didn't even know where Shane was.

Justin leaned back. "Who would've thought? The Eternal Couple."

"Guess nobody's going to be saying that anymore."

"I'm sorry. But maybe this is better for them."

"But how can they?" She finally turned to look at Justin. "I can't believe it. No matter how miserable they made each other, no matter what people said, they always stayed together. Why are they doing this now? If they wanted to divorce, they should've done it years ago while they still had time to start fresh. What's the point?"

"Who knows what they're thinking? Maybe they were waiting until you guys were all grown. Maybe they decided it's better to live freely now than never."

She turned away and wiped away a tear. Justin handed her a box of tissues. "They still should've done it years ago." Before the whole family lived through decades of misery. Before she found all those letters in the vanity drawer in her mother's bedroom.

Justin silently put a hand on her shoulder. When the delivery guy came with the food, he paid and came over to spread the Chinese all over the low coffee table. He served the beef and broccoli and Peking duck—her favorite. She didn't think it was a coincidence given how much he disliked broccoli.

She tilted her head, trying to figure him out. There was something matter-of-fact about the way he moved and talked, like everything that had happened between them in November didn't even exist. "Why are you being so nice to me?"

A beat of silence, then Justin answered, "Iain asked me." He pushed a plate her way and handed her a pair of chopsticks. "Eat."

She pushed the food around, then finally nibbled on a broccoli floret when Justin gave her a cool, steady stare. It tasted great, and she realized she was actually quite hungry. "He called?"

Justin nodded and started eating. There was something very methodical and driven about the way he ate. He didn't shovel his food down like some men she knew, but he didn't take his time either. It reminded her of somebody trying to eat an entire elephant without making himself sick—one bite at a time, chew, swallow, repeat at a steady speed until he was finished.

They ate in a silence that wasn't too awkward. "You should've told him you were too busy," she said after the final piece of duck.

He poured two glasses of claret and pushed one her way, and she let herself smile a bit while rolling the stem. This was so like him—keeping his promise without her having to prompt him. She breathed in the wine—the luscious black currant scent—and took a small sip, unable to wait.

"The real question is: why did you come to Chicago? You don't have any friends here."

The priceless vintage turned bitter in her mouth, and she forced herself to swallow. "Would you believe me if I told you the flight to Chicago happened to be the earliest one out of L.A.?"

He snorted, swirling the wine in his glass. "Are you really a successful attorney? Hard to imagine, when you lie so poorly."

They'd dated on and off for over ten years. Somehow he seemed to know everything about her, while her family seemed clueless about what she was up to half the time.

Vanessa finished her wine. She didn't know what made her keep coming back to him. They should've quit each other after she'd finished law school. She'd told him so. Even broken up with him. But then that wasn't how it'd happened. They'd kept calling, kept seeing each other, kept having sex.

And that wasn't like her. She'd never once clung to a guy she'd decided to break up with, but with Justin she was unable to control herself.

"I came to Chicago because I had nobody else

to turn to." She drank more of the wine and laughed a sad laugh. "That didn't sound as pathetic when I thought it in my head."

Placing his empty glass on the table, Justin leaned forward. "It doesn't sound pathetic. It actually sounds lonely."

Vanessa bit her lower lip. This was what made him so difficult to ignore…and impossible to be with. He could see through all the smiles and outer shells and artifices. Nobody understood her the way he did, and he made her want things that would only bring her misery in the end.

She drained her glass. She no longer felt cold, but she kept his coat around her anyway.

"You're so contradictory and unpredictable," he said. "If I didn't know you so well, I would've thought you were playing games."

Her face heated. "I'm not…" She cringed as the argument from November flashed through her mind. "I'm sorry about all this." She waved her hand vaguely. "I know you're angry with me."

"Angry isn't quite the right word."

She winced. Most assuredly not. More like furious…maybe even murderous. She doubted any other man would have come pick her up at the airport, even as a favor to one of his closest friends.

Tilting her chin up with an index finger, Justin lowered his head until their breaths mingled. "'Angry' is simple. One dimensional. What I'm feeling right now is a little more complicated than that."

Her mouth dried, and her heart beat harder and faster against her ribcage. Justin smelled amazing, like pine forest and man, and his dark eyes seemed to suck her right into him.

She didn't know why she wasn't pulling back from him. If nothing else, pride and self-preservation should've made her get the hell out of Justin's condo. Hadn't she been glad when he'd broken things off? She'd told herself he was being unreasonable and melodramatic, and that she wasn't going to go to him first.

But right now she wanted to be close to him. All through her adult life, Justin had been an anchor that never changed. If she clung to him, nothing would be able to sweep her away.

She closed the distance between them. His lips were firm under hers, unresponsive. She pulled him closer, both hands on the back of his head, and opened up, tracing her tongue over the flat line of his mouth.

The longer he remained passive, the more aggressive she became, channeling her pain into the desperate act of kissing him. She didn't want him to remain angry with her. She wanted him to know how sorry she was for being unfair to him and how much she appreciated his support. Just being there for her was huge. Her parents' divorce was really unsettling, and she couldn't even say why. She felt like one of those helpless kids she represented pro bono.

She rested her palm over his heart and felt its movement, like a fish caught in a net. *Forgive me, Justin. Forgive me…*

Finally some of the tension went out of him, and his hands traveled up her sides as he began to kiss her back. Relief and exhilaration flooded her. She shed his coat, let it glide over her and pool by the couch.

He pulled her into his lap and dug a hand into her hair, ruining the way she'd set it. She deepened the kiss, adjusting herself so she was seated with her sex flush against his erection.

He licked the small mole on her neck. "I don't know why I can't say no to you." His breath was hot against her skin. "It should be easy to say no."

"I'm glad you can't. Because I can't say no to you either."

THREE

JUSTIN CURSED UNDER HIS BREATH. WHEN Vanessa was like this, it was like all the hurtful words had never been spoken. He went weak for her even though he knew how bad she was. If any of his friends had had the kind of relationship he had with Vanessa, he would've advised them to get the hell out.

But none of that mattered when she was in front of him like this.

He pulled the flimsy blouse out of her skirt and unbuttoned it. She unhooked her bra and tossed it on the floor. Need thrummed deep inside his belly at the sight of her. He wanted to tell himself it was only because he hadn't had sex since they'd broken up, but that would be a lie. Even if he'd had a dozen orgasms the night before, he'd still be hot for her.

"Justin..."

He undressed her the rest of the way, then carried her to the bedroom and placed her on his bed. Her crimson hair spread around her like fire. The sight of her there stroked a deep, primal urge in him. For the first time, she was in *his* bed. Hotel beds had their appeal, but this was more.

His fingers moved on auto-pilot. His shirt buttons came undone, cuff links dropped into a small crystal bowl in the closet. Shoes and socks disappeared, and his slacks and underwear vanished.

Vanessa's eyes never left his body as he undressed. A deep flush tinted her cheeks, and her pupils grew impossibly wide and dark.

He moved over her, tracing the smooth curves of her calves and thighs. Her breath hitched as his fingers traveled upward, then he stopped, blowing gently at the black curls between her legs. She was already wet.

He dropped a soft kiss on her belly. "You look perfect."

"So do you."

With a little smile, he kissed and licked along her legs. They were lean and trim from daily jogging, and he loved their shape and strength.

He gently ran a finger along the seam at the juncture of her thighs. She was scorching hot and wet. He put her juices on his tongue and groaned at the pure honeyed taste.

Propping her legs on his shoulders, he feasted on her. Her back arched at the feel of his tongue, and he hummed with satisfaction at how responsive she was. Maybe her firm had kept her so busy since November that she hadn't had a free moment to think about another man, much less actually get laid.

Jealousy spiked, but he kicked it down. This wasn't the time. Vanessa was in his bed, moaning under his mouth.

He swirled his tongue over her clit and pushed his finger into her. Her inner muscles clutched at him, and he groaned at how responsive she was as he moved it in and out of her in that erratic rhythm she liked so much.

As much as he wanted to draw the moment out, he couldn't wait much longer. His cock throbbed with the need to be inside her, and he wanted her limp and pliable from a powerful orgasm before he entered her.

Her hands twisted the sheet, and her breathing took on a staccatoed, panicked tone, like she was afraid he'd abandon her now when she was so close. He didn't understand why; he'd never left her unsatisfied.

"Justin!" His name on her lips was the sweetest sound ever. He kept up the pressure as she rode wave after wave of the first of many orgasms he planned to give her that night. She was so beautiful, abandoning herself to the pleasure.

Finally she brought him up for a deep kiss. He lay over her, anticipating what was to come, and his cock grew even harder. She reached between their bodies and ran her index finger over the slick blunt tip of his erection, then put it in her mouth. "Mmmm. Yummy."

"Wicked," Justin murmured.

"And I live in L.A."

"The wicked wench of the west."

She laughed, the sound husky. Then she whispered into his ear, "Less talk, more action."

VANESSA SMILED WHEN JUSTIN GAVE INTO HIS NEED and trailed his lips along her neck, his hands traveling over her torso, moving closer and closer to her breasts. He made her feel so free in bed, like she could do or say anything and it would be all right. Maybe that was what kept their time together so fresh and hot. Nothing else could explain why she still wanted him like this after ten years of an on-and-off relationship.

Justin's firm hand cupped her breast with exactly the right amount of pressure, making her draw a sharp breath at how amazing it felt.

He flicked his finger over her aching nipple, and she clenched her inner muscles as she grew slick between her legs.

He took his time with her breast. Where was he getting the patience? She could feel his cock throbbing against her. She licked her lips. She wanted him inside her probably more than he wanted to plunge into her.

Finally he pulled her nipple into his mouth, trapping the hard point between the roof of his mouth and tongue. The edge of his teeth scraped against the soft skin, and she tunneled her fingers through his silky hair as desire heated rapidly in her belly, like she hadn't just had a powerful orgasm.

When he finally released her breast, she kissed him and rolled him over. As he watched her, she got on her knees and gripped the headboard. Then very deliberately, she spread her thighs and arched her back.

He nuzzled the gentle slopes of her buttocks, his hot breath fanning over her heated skin. She pushed herself toward him, and he stroked her clit. "You're gorgeous like this." He nipped her, sending a sharp tang of want along her spine. "Good enough to eat."

"No more talking. Show me."

With a soft laugh, he opened a drawer by his bed and put on a condom. Once protected, he gripped her pelvis and pushed into her, delicious inch by delicious inch.

She bit her lower lip at the sweet invasion, the way he stretched and filled her. When he was hilted, she moaned. It was incredible how having his cock inside her could make her feel so connected to him. "Justin…"

He pumped his lean hips, moving in and out of her in a rhythm she found irresistible. As the pleasure built, her lips parted in a silent cry. Something close to fear slid over her mind at how vulnerable and open she was to Justin right now. A small part of her wanted to pull back, but she couldn't. The pleasure he gave her was so addicting, she was helpless to deny him.

Justin reached around and rubbed her clit. "Come for me."

"Yes!" She screamed his name as a powerful orgasm consumed her. It was like being electrocuted with pleasure, and she felt like she would black out from the intensity of it.

His grip tightened as he thrust into her with more power and speed. She hung on to the headboard for dear life. He shouted as he climaxed, his body taut and strong.

She turned to watch him over her shoulder. He looked so primal with pleasure twisting his handsome face, and she held back a secret smile of satisfaction at knowing that she was the cause.

Some time later when his breathing slowed, he got up and went to the bathroom. Afterward, he returned to bed and wrapped his arm around her. Spooning her, he pressed his face against the back of her neck. "Spend the night with me. I'll have my pilot take you to L.A. in the morning."

She linked fingers with him, then waited until his body grew lax with sleep. There were so many reasons why she should leave…and just one reason why she should stay. But that reason seemed to trump all the others.

She turned to watch his face as he slept. Justin was just too perfect. She should never have come to Chicago or slept with him, no matter how right it'd felt. No other man had ever given her that panicked sensation of total vulnerability, whereas Justin never failed to arouse it.

If she wasn't careful, he might take up a permanent spot in her mind. And that wouldn't do. She knew what happened when people let themselves become that exposed.

Seven hours later, Justin woke up alone in bed. There was a small memo on the bedside table, and he reached for it.

Thanks for everything.
– V

He didn't have to get up to make sure she was gone. It was a typical Vanessa post-coital good-bye. A fist over his eyes, he cursed. He really needed to get a woman who was better for him. This gut twisting feeling Vanessa gave him simply wasn't good. And he was getting tired of the whole messed up hot-and-cold thing they had going, no matter how irresistible it was.

If a business associate had treated him like this, he would've cut the person out of his life instantly. Personal affairs weren't exactly like business, but maybe he should make an exception for Vanessa. After all, hadn't he learned that nothing was absolute, how there was an exception to everything?

Decision made, he sat up and scrolled through the huge list of women on his phone. Then he found the number and dialed.

VANESSA STUFFED THE PANIC AWAY AS SHE returned to her office from the bathroom. Still no period, and she wasn't feeling even the slightest bit of premenstrual cramp.

The most she'd ever been late was one week. It had been five weeks since she'd left Justin's bed.

"Are you all right?" her secretary Zoe said, looking up from her laptop screen with a newsfeed scrolling on the bottom. Something about some reality TV show star getting pregnant. "You look a little pale."

"I'm fine."

Zoe's middle-aged face pinched, deepening the wrinkles around her eyes and mouth. "They're working you too hard. A hundred and twenty is much too much."

Vanessa flashed the smile she always gave people who worried about her working too much. "Don't let the partners hear you say that."

She closed the door to her office and sat behind her desk. A mountain of documents related to Solaris Med demanded her attention, but she couldn't focus on anything. She hadn't been sleeping well, and she'd been busy. Like Zoe had said, a hundred and twenty hours might actually be too much, and that would explain why she hadn't had a period in five weeks.

Instead of trying to come up with wishful reasons why she wasn't having her period—menopause was not a plausible explanation—she picked up her purse. She had to know. "Zoe, I'll be gone for an hour or so."

"But you have a conference with Felix," she said.

Oh crap. That was right. They were supposed to discuss the sexual harassment case and strategy. "Can you reschedule? Tell him I'm sorry."

"Okay." Zoe frowned, her dark eyes owlish behind rimless glasses.

There was a drug store not too far from the office. She bought a pregnancy test and went into the bathroom at the back of the store. After following the instructions, she stared at her slim watch as the seconds ticked by. She couldn't be pregnant… she just couldn't…

She glanced at the result box on the stick, and all the air whooshed out of her. She put a hand on the stall door for support as her knees turned to pudding.

She was.

FOUR

"Have you heard? Kerri's pregnant."

Justin looked up from a pile of documents as his great-uncle Barron walked into his living room on a Saturday. "What? No. Congratulations."

"I imagine it's a boy."

Barron took a seat without waiting for an invitation and pulled out a box of sugar cookies and a tumbler full of Earl Gray tea. They were his favorite, but he knew Justin didn't keep any at home.

Despite his age, Barron looked as solid as ever, glowing with good health. If Justin hadn't known better, he might've thought Barron had found an elixir of eternal youth. As usual, he wore a bespoke suit, hand-tailored in Europe. The dark navy of the silk looked good on him. His watch flashed on his wrist. It was an old, inexpensive piece, but he'd never thrown away any of his late wife's presents.

Justin was happy for his cousin, but at the same time a sharp envy formed in his gut. It seemed like everyone was with the one they wanted to be with except him. And he hated this pathetic, lousy feeling of jealousy and self-pity. Neither was like him. *Damn you, Vanessa.*

"How far along is she?" Justin asked, forcing a small smile. Nobody needed to know about his personal problems. He'd already made up his mind to move on.

"Only six weeks." He held up an index finger. "But I have a hunch about this child."

Justin nodded, leaning back in his seat. "What can I do for you, Barron?"

His great-uncle wouldn't have flown all the way to Chicago just to talk about Kerri's pregnancy. As much as Barron adored his granddaughter, he was a busy man, busier now with a new-found love. Shocking that he actually felt something for another human being. More shocking that a woman actually genuinely liked him. Most of the women who'd buzzed around him did so because they wanted his money and influence.

Barron pulled out a sugar cookie. "When are you going to produce a child?"

Justin suppressed a sigh. *This again.* "When I find a woman who wants me, not my money."

The older man snorted. "I'm surprised none of your exes thought to get pregnant. That would've been the easiest way to get you to marry them."

"Child support is cheaper and infinitely preferable. Besides, I'm sure our lawyers would win the custody battle."

"They better, given how much they're paid." Barron expected the very best from everyone who worked for him—that was to say, to give him everything he wanted when he wanted it.

"If that's all—"

"If you don't find a wife soon, I plan to find one for you."

"Please, no matchmaking."

"There are heiresses who wouldn't want your money."

"How many who are worth twenty-five billion?" Justin steepled his fingers. "You know how it is. No limit on greed."

Barron sighed. "You know why I groomed you myself, don't you? To carry on the family legacy. Grow it, for subsequent generations."

Justin nodded.

"And that means you have certain responsibilities to me, as well as to the family. One of which is that you marry and produce an heir whom you can groom yourself. I'd like to see this before I die."

"If you ever die. I swear you're going to outlive us all."

Barron laughed his booming laugh. "You say that now, but I'm not young anymore. I'll die soon enough. I mean what I said, Justin. Marry that London girl you're with."

Justin narrowed his eyes. London Bickham had a sizable trust fund, and she was funny and nice, but she sometimes bored him. Still, she was a good distraction to help him forget Vanessa.

"Don't give me that look. London's a good girl. Pretty too."

The intercom buzzed, thankfully giving Justin a small reprieve. It was London.

"Speak of the devil." Barron smiled, his eyes twinkling.

"We have a lunch date," Justin said.

"When I was your age, I picked the girl up at her house."

"She's a modern woman. Has her own driver's license and everything."

A few minutes later the elevator doors opened, London strolled in. Many assumed it was her golden hair and wide blue eyes that made her look like a child's doll, but Justin disagreed. It was her eyes, completely devoid of intellect or a single original thought. Still, he preferred his rebound to be the polar opposite of Vanessa.

London's hips swayed, making the hem of her pale green dress swirl around her thighs. Her unbound curls cascaded over her slim shoulders, and she didn't show any surprise at the sight of

Barron. "Hello, Justin. Barron, I didn't know you were going to be in Chicago."

"Don't mind me." He brushed invisible cookie crumbs from his clothes.

"Are you joining us for lunch?"

"No. I have to return to Maryland."

London smiled blankly at Barron, while Justin relaxed. Maryland meant only one thing—he was going back to Stella Lloyd, the new love of his life. Justin made a mental note to send her a big basket of gourmet European chocolate and flowers. Barron was technically retired, but in actuality he was semi-retired, always nosing around at Sterling & Wilson. It had the unfortunate side effect of undermining Justin at times. But ever since Barron had met Stella, he'd been too busy in Maryland to drive Justin insane, and for that the woman deserved a lifetime of chocolate and flowers.

"You two lovebirds have a good time," Barron said, heaving himself up and leaving.

"He's so sweet," London said.

Justin hid a cool smile. "He's not bad."

Most people who'd ever worked for or with him would never call Barron "sweet." He was a faithful disciple of Machiavelli—make people fear you and crush them when they mess with you so they could never rise up against you, ever. And unlike Justin, Barron was fully capable of applying it to everyone, including his own family.

After putting on a coat, Justin placed a hand at the small of London's back. She smelled heavily of a pricey perfume, nothing at all like Vanessa, who rarely wore any. "Shall we go?"

Five weeks and two days of not seeing Vanessa Pryce. After a year or two, he might stop thinking about her.

TAKING A DEEP BREATH, VANESSA PARKED HER rental in front of Justin's condo. She needed to get out of the car, but fear and apprehension kept her stuck in her seat. She didn't know how to start the conversation. Amazing really, when you thought about it—as a lawyer she wasn't exactly the tongue-tied type. But Justin wasn't an opposing counsel or a hostile witness.

The clouds sat dark and heavy, their bodies swollen with impending rain. Vanessa hoped the rain would hold off until she returned to the airport for her flight later.

What if Justin refused to see her?

Every kid needed a father. Vanessa had seen what the absence of one could do from the pro-bono work she did. Even Salazar had always been there for her and her brothers, while preoccupied with chasing every pretty face he saw. And she knew Justin would love his child.

She'd been so cowardly the last time they'd met. Sneaking out like a juvenile had been foolish, but she'd panicked when she'd woken in the pre-dawn light and realized she didn't want to leave.

Rumor had it that Justin was dating London Bickham now. For the first time since Vanessa had broken up with him in Vegas, he'd been with someone for over a month. Still, she couldn't help but wonder what Justin saw in her. As pretty as the heiress was, she could make a Valley Girl seem like Marie Curie by comparison.

Maybe I should've texted first to set up an appointment. They'd never socialized in public or barged in on each other's lives unannounced. Well, that wasn't technically true. She'd shown up five weeks ago. And they'd interacted briefly when he'd visited her office last November. How her coworkers had talked!

Vanessa's going to be a partner no matter what. Did you see how Justin Sterling looked at and talked to her? You don't think the partners noticed?

Her jaw tightened. When she made partner it would be on her own merit, not because of who her family and friends were.

She pulled her hat lower, then made sure the face net covered her properly. Her red hair was pulled tightly and most of it was hidden under the hat. The black dress was something her mother might wear, but she didn't care. She wanted to make sure she was difficult to recognize…and unapproachable.

Feeling like a stalker, she stepped out of her rental. The March Chicago wind nipped at her. She shivered, pulling her long, black coat closer. No matter how she prepared herself, the chill of the Chicago winter never failed to surprise her. She wished she had Justin's coat around her again, then shook herself. This was why she shouldn't be with him. This pathetic needy side of her was unwelcome, appalling.

As she locked her car, a couple of familiar figures emerged out of the condo. She stopped and looked. It was Justin and London.

They made a handsome couple. Justin's dark head was lowered, and he whispered something in London's ear. The blonde's laughter rang out, bright and merry. Justin placed a hand on her shoulder, and she leaned into him.

Vanessa's hands shook as another image superimposed itself over the view in front of her.

Her father Salazar's head dipping, a blonde in his arms laughing at something he'd said… They'd left a downtown hotel together as Vanessa watched. She'd been six at the time, but she'd understood what the woman meant—a betrayal of her mother. By the time she'd been born, nobody was bothering to hide what her dad was up to. And when she was a few years older, she'd realized what they'd been doing in the hotel room.

Uncertainty bled into misery. She should just leave, before anybody noticed her. She should—

"Vanessa!"

She flinched at the high-pitched squeal. London rushed over to her. "Oh my gosh, *look* at you! What are you doing in Chicago?"

"Meeting some friends," Vanessa said smoothly.

Justin followed London over. His eyes had gone as cold as the wind.

Ignoring him, Vanessa cleared her throat. "You look great, London."

"Thanks. Justin and I were about to go to lunch. Wanna join us?" She turned to Justin. "Wouldn't that be great?"

He didn't look at Vanessa. "I'm sure she's busy, dear."

Vanessa pasted on a smile. "Very." She made a show of looking at her watch. "In fact, my flight's leaving in less than two hours."

"Oh, darn. You know what? We'll do lunch next time I'm in L.A.," London said.

"Of course," Vanessa said. "Well, gotta go." She slipped into her car before she lost her composure completely and told Justin why she was in Chicago in front of his girlfriend. Then with more force than necessary, she yanked on her seatbelt and stomped on the gas.

JUSTIN WATCHED VANESSA'S MAROON TAURUS DISappear into the Chicago traffic. What the hell. London seemed to have bought Vanessa's story about work in the city, but he didn't. Why was she back in Chicago?

If it was for another night of sex, she could forget it. He was doing quite well on his detox program.

Still…

There had been dark half-circles under the layers of careful eye makeup. And her face had seemed paler than usual, her cheekbones more prominent. *Probably working herself to death.*

She'd been unusually tense as she'd spoken with London, and if it had been any other woman he might have considered it jealousy. But Vanessa Pryce never felt jealousy over a man. The only thing she cared about was her career, "making partner." It'd become an obsession during her law school years, although he didn't understand why. It wasn't like she needed the money. If she wanted to be a law firm partner, she could've just created her own. That would be the easiest way, given her background and financial situation. It didn't have to be at her current law firm.

"Justin, are you all right?" London asked.

He blinked and looked down at the petite heiress. "Sorry. Thinking about a new project." He forced a smile. "Let's go."

He was going to get through week five and day two of his Vanessa detox program.

FIVE

THE RAIN POURED DOWN AS THOUGH SOMEbody had slit the clouds' fat bellies. No matter what setting she used for the wipers, Vanessa couldn't see anything in front of her. There was no way she was going to reach O'Hare in weather like this.

She pulled over and stared outside. Shudders went through her every time a car sped by, making her rental rock. It didn't look like the rain would let up any time soon. There wasn't even a sliver of blue on the dark horizon. She pulled out her phone to check the weather in Chicago. *Rain for the rest of the day. Great.*

Maybe she should just call Mark and ask him to arrange for a pickup. Her brother would do it, and unlike Iain he wouldn't ask annoying questions. She didn't want to discuss why she was in Chicago with anybody. Her business was strictly with Justin.

She pressed her head against the headrest and tapped the edge of her phone. Maybe she didn't have to tell Justin. It wasn't like she wanted him to get involved with her life. He seemed to have moved on, and it looked like London might be the one for him, given how long they'd been dating.

And the idea of him being with London—or any woman—twisted her heart. Vanessa rubbed her forehead. When had she turned into a dog in a manger? It wasn't like she was going to start dating him if he just ditched everyone else.

She put a hand over her belly. Even if she wanted to keep it quiet, this wasn't something she could hide…not to mention the child would want to know about its father.

Before she lost her nerve, she typed *I'm pregnant* and hit send. As soon as her phone showed "sent" confirmation, she cursed. What the hell had she been thinking? This was what happened when she was tired and sleep-deprived and stressed.

She checked the settings on her phone. There had to be a way to recall that text before Justin saw it.

Nobody needed to know whose baby she carried. She could just say she didn't know, and it wasn't like she needed anybody's approval. She made her own money, and she had an amazing career. She could raise the baby on her own, and it would never lack for anything, even if it didn't have the Sterling family's level of wealth.

Money wasn't everything in life.

She stared at the phone. No response from Justin. Maybe he didn't see it. Maybe he'd lost his phone or changed his number.

Or he might just laugh it off. He'd probably think she'd sent it by error or something. They'd been so careful, always using birth control. He would think it was a prank, a bad one, but prank nonetheless.

Weren't there dozens of reason why she shouldn't be with him anyway, even if London hadn't been in the picture? He was too handsome, too sexy, too good in bed, too popular, too rich and too likely to influence her career. But most importantly, he was too likely to break her heart. She knew herself. If she stayed with him for too long, she'd fall for him and nothing—not even love—was enough to make relationships last.

She looked at the water streaming down her windshield. The rain would let up at some point. When it was light enough for her to drive again, she'd either make her way to the airport or check into a nearby hotel.

Whichever was safer.

JUSTIN SMILED AT LONDON. SHE'D BEEN CHATTERing about shoes for the last half-hour. She had to be an alien whose mind and logic defied human understanding. What else could explain her obsessive desire to talk about leather used to make shoes in Italy?

The lobster bisque was unexpectedly excellent and provided great distraction from the monologue. Rain ran down the windows in rivulets, and he took a brief glance at the wet pavement. Was Vanessa going to be okay driving to the airport? She was a prototypical Californian—the most inclement weather she could stand was cloudy.

"So what do you think?" London asked, jerking his attention back.

He managed a smile. "I think it's great." *A great non-answer*, guilt needled him. He shouldn't care about Vanessa's driving in the rain. What she did wasn't any of his concern. He was on a date with a woman who actually liked having a relationship with him, and she didn't slice away a bit of his heart every time they met. But somehow his mind rebelled at being in the restaurant, and he controlled his breathing. Vanessa was like a bottle of booze to a recovering alcoholic. One sip and he was done for.

When his phone buzzed in his pocket, he excused himself to check it. Anything to delay London from launching into the merits of stilettos.

His mood grew as dark as the weather outside when he noticed a text from Vanessa. He should delete it. It was probably something that would upset him. Or tempt him.

But he recalled her pallor. She'd looked absolutely wretched and tired, and he'd never seen her like that. Was her parents' divorce weighing her down? She was close to her mother, and he knew the situation with her parents had always bothered her. Even though their marriage had been a joke of cosmic proportions, everyone had assumed Salazar and Ceinlys Pryce would always stay married to each other.

Cursing himself, he thumbed the screen. Then blinked.

I'm pregnant.

His heart thumped, and the words jumbled in his mind. It couldn't be…

He stared at the text again, willing it to make sense. But no. It was still the same two words.

His body went slack. Now he understood why she'd been at his place. She probably wanted to talk about the baby. He remembered how she'd smiled her lawyer smile at London and climbed into her car as soon as possible without appearing rude. What else could she have done with the other woman there?

Closing his eyes, he let out a soft sigh. So many thoughts tumbled through his mind, but one thing was clear. He couldn't let her go now.

"London, I'm sorry, but it's an emergency. Do you mind?"

"No, not at all," she said. "Business?"

"Something like that. I'll call you a car."

"You're so sweet." She smiled at him, her eyes semi-vacant now that they were no longer talking about shoes. "Thanks."

Her simple understanding made him feel lower than dirt. She might not be the most brilliant or interesting woman he knew, but she was one of the sweetest. He couldn't continue to sit with her and fake-laugh and fake-talk his way through the lunch. She deserved better.

And he and Vanessa were having a baby.

He took care of the meal and climbed into his Bentley. He dialed Vanessa's number, but she didn't pick up. Damn it.

Grinding his teeth, he texted Vanessa. *Where are you?*

A little bit later, he got a response. *Did you see the text I sent you earlier?*

Yes.

That was a mistake. I meant to send it to somebody else.

He snorted. *Who? I wanna send onesies.* When she didn't respond, he scowled. *Vanessa, if you don't tell me where you are, I'm going to get the cops out looking for you.*

You wouldn't.

I can and I will. Guess who's on my speed dial? Not to mention the tons of money he'd donated to the memorial funds and others for Chicago's finest.

I'm pulled over on I-90. Other than that, no idea where I am.

Stay right there. Justin instructed his driver to take I-90 toward O'Hare and look for a maroon Taurus on the shoulder.

It didn't take that long to find Vanessa's rental. It had the emergency blinkers on. Thank god she couldn't drive in the rain. Otherwise she would've left the city by now. In Los Angeles she was a speed demon.

Justin jumped out of his car and ran to it before his driver could bring out the umbrella. The icy rain soaked him instantly, and he pounded on the passenger door. Vanessa unlocked it.

"You're going to ruin the seat," she said, staring straight out the windshield. Her voice was tight.

"I don't give a damn."

She sniffled. The obvious signs of fatigue and her loss of weight hit him again, but this time they took on another dimension.

"Are you eating and sleeping well?" he asked, trying not to show his exasperation. "You know, all those things pregnant women should do."

"Of course."

She was lying through her teeth. Knowing her, she probably did billable work in her dreams too.

"The baby's the reason why you came to see me," Justin said.

"I didn't. I don't even know what made me text that."

"Really."

"You aren't even going to question whether it's really yours?"

"Who else's could it be?" She wouldn't have texted him if it wasn't his.

Her throat worked. "It doesn't change anything."

"How can you say that?"

"Justin, go back to the restaurant. It's not nice to ditch your girlfriend in the middle of lunch. If you want"—she finally turned to face him—"I'll draw up some papers releasing you from parental responsibilities."

He reined in his temper. "What kind of man do you think I am? You think I'm worried about paying child support?"

"It's not about you." Her shoulders slumped for a moment, but she squared them, her mouth tight now. "Unscrupulous women generally demand more."

Except Vanessa wasn't unscrupulous. She probably wished she'd never come to Chicago or told him she was pregnant. She obviously didn't want him involved, as though he had nothing to do with the baby they'd created.

"No," he said. "It's my baby. I'll be a father to it."

"Justin, you don't have to. Whoever you end up marrying won't like it that you have a child with somebody else."

"Remarkable, that you know so much about this woman," he said sarcastically. It was either that or blow up on her as she spoke of him marrying another woman while she was carrying his baby.

"I'm a lawyer, remember? When you have the kind of money you do, people always think way, way ahead. To the estate. It's not cynicism, it's reality."

"You're right."

"Thank you."

"There's only one thing left for us to do." He smiled, watching her eyes narrow. "Get married."

VANESSA SUCKED IN A BREATH. "DEFINITELY NOT. I didn't tell you so you'd marry me."

"So it's something else then?"

"Look, I just...didn't want this to be a surprise later on. I know what something like that can do to a family."

"You're referring to your stepbrother?"

She nodded. Her father had a son with another woman and had brought him into the fold. Vanessa didn't have any hard feelings against Blaine, since it wasn't his fault Salazar was a womanizer. Ceinlys had been absolutely furious, of course, and Vanessa suspected it had added another dimension to her mother's sudden desire to divorce.

"Salazar didn't do the right thing because he was already married. I'm not."

"Justin—"

"Don't make me fight you over this. If it goes public, it won't be just me after you."

"What do you mean?"

"Barron has been after me to marry and 'produce an heir.' Well, this baby is it. Heir to the Sterling & Wilson fortune."

Vanessa bit her lower lip. "I want to keep our marriage quiet."

"Quiet?"

"*Quiet*. Undercover, on the sly, in secret. Get it done outside the country or something."

The muscles in his jaw flexed. "I'm not going to continue what we've been doing the last ten years. We're talking about *marriage* here."

"It's important."

"Why?"

Because it's going to end soon…and badly, she thought. Justin couldn't even pretend he felt anything that was strong enough to compel him to suggest matrimony to her. Her parents had loved each other to pieces, and their marriage had eventually become a train wreck. The divorce was going to be just as bad with a bunch of over-priced lawyers squabbling over every penny.

Justin was her kryptonite, and unlike Superman she was too stupid to stay away from him. One day when she least expected it, he'd destroy her. And probably the child too. She put a hand over her belly. Children were always collateral damage in their parents' battles.

She dropped her gaze to stare at the bottom of the steering wheel. "I don't want who you are to affect my career."

"I don't see how it's related."

He had to be joking, but maybe he honestly didn't get it. Everyone knew he'd been hand-picked by his great-uncle to lead Sterling & Wilson. He'd been groomed from a very early age to be what he was today, and nobody whispered that the only reason he'd become Barron's heir was dumb luck or anything other than his hard work and intellect.

"If I were a man," Vanessa began, "who I was married to wouldn't be a big deal. But for women, it is more important than what they accomplish. When a woman is discussed in a professional capacity, they talk about her marital status, whether or not she has children. If she's pregnant, they discuss whether or not she's taking maternity leave. It's sexist and unfair, but that's the way it is, and I have to work within that."

She could never forget what Dane had said: *It's not like they're hiring you for your brain. You can probably make partner without winning a single case, so long as you give them the Pryce family business.*

She'd rather die than prove Dane right.

"If you're worried about maternity leave..."

"It's not the leave. If people see that I'm married to you, they're going to wonder how much your name has affected the kind of cases, performance evaluations and raises I get. I made it clear to my firm from the beginning that I would never bring my family's business to them, and I've worked very hard to nip any hint of favoritism at the bud. And so far, I think it's worked. But you're different." She raised her chin. "When I make partner, it's going to be based on my professional accomplishments, not because I'm married to you."

"You've been at the firm for ten years, right?"

She nodded.

"I'll wait until July. That's when you have your eval, right?"

Her eyes widened. "How did you know?"

"You mentioned it once. I'll wait until then, and if you make partner, great. If not..." He shrugged. "I won't wait beyond that."

"But—"

"No buts. This is non-negotiable." His eyes were cold, and his tone even colder. She'd never seen him like this before, and his hard expression killed her objections. "You won't be able to hide your pregnancy by then anyway. And we'll be living together as a couple." He put a finger on the tip of her nose. "Discreetly."

"I'm not moving to Chicago," she said quickly before she lost all control of the situation.

He shrugged. "That's fine. I can be in L.A."

"You don't have an office in L.A." Sterling & Wilson's California office was in San Francisco.

"*I* am Sterling & Wilson, not some building." There was a quiet surety and confidence in his voice.

Her mouth dried. "Are we going to Vegas?"

"Nothing as clichéd as that. Take next Friday off. I'll send a jet to pick you up in the morning."

"If you tell me where we're going, I can arrange for my own trans—"

"Don't. I'm meeting you most of the way, Vanessa. So humor me on this. Also we should go back to my place and get you fed and rested."

"Can't. I have tons of work to do, and I don't want another associate to suffer because I'm not pulling my weight."

"Felix Peck?"

She nodded.

"Fine. I'll send you home on my jet then. And don't even think about driving in this weather." He pulled out a credit card and handed it to her. "Put whatever you need on this."

She stared at the black AmEx. This was too fast, and panic knotted her belly. "What about London?" she said, desperate to throw up whatever obstacle she could manage.

"I'll take care of her. All you need to do is show up."

SIX

SITTING IN ONE OF THE CONFERENCE ROOMS AT Highsmith, Dickson and Associates, Vanessa checked her phone again. Justin had to have gotten her text that morning, but so far there was no answer.

Sighing, she pushed the thoughts of Justin out of her mind and tried to concentrate on the mountain of papers in front of her. She needed to review them all. The opposing counsel was being a jerk. Apparently he'd decided to kill her with kindness by sending her every minute document.

Soon Felix strolled in with two Starbucks and a paper bag filled with fries. A Yale graduate, he reminded Vanessa of a hungry lion with burning dark eyes and brown hair streaked with golden highlights. His thin lips looked like he disapproved of everyone, especially when he set them in an unsmiling line. They worked wonders when he wanted to intimidate witnesses or difficult clients.

As usual, Felix was in another of his classic Armani outfits, although he'd dressed on the casual side for the weekend. Unlike Vanessa, he had come from a lower middle class family in Cincinnati, and he was extra aware of the image he needed to project even though he didn't mind food slumming with her on difficult cases. In return, Vanessa hooked him up at La Mer or Éternité, two of the most exclusive restaurants in the city owned by her brother Mark.

"You sure you don't want to take some time off this weekend?" Felix said, handing her her tea. "You look like hell."

"No, but thank you for the compliment."

"You know what I mean."

Vanessa knew exactly what he meant. She looked and *felt* like hell. Apparently crackers didn't agree with her, and now she was craving French fries with the heat of a thousand suns. "I'm a little behind. Besides, I have tons of work to do before next Friday."

"I can't believe Harry gave you another day off," he said, taking his seat. "I was sure he'd say no. What's the secret?"

"It's conditional." Dickson had made it clear if she got everything done by Thursday, she could take

Friday off. Otherwise, she had to keep her ass in her seat and get the work done.

"Yeah, right!" Stan Rivers stuck his head through the open door and snorted. "You'll be able to go even if you don't finish anything. Everyone knows that."

Vanessa gave him a long, hard stare. A couple of years older than her, Stan was the most likely associate to make partner next, although there was some whispering that Vanessa might take his spot. She hated how people tried to pit them against each other, but most importantly she hated how smug and annoying Stan was. He was always bringing up the fact that she was a Pryce girl and knew a lot of people. He even talked about how she'd been invited to Barron Sterling's granddaughter's wedding—in a not so subtle way—to hint that she was being promoted at the firm only because of her connections.

It was just her luck he wasn't even a terrible lawyer. He wasn't great, but he was better than average—good enough to survive at the firm. Plus he knew how to be slick with partners and clients. He always dressed well and swaggered around like he knew he was a shoo-in for the promotion.

Which made her jaw ache.

"If I had the influence you think I do, you wouldn't be working here." Vanessa reached for her fries. "Felix, do you mind shutting the door? We have a lot of *billable*"—she looked pointedly at the pile of documents to review—"work to do."

With an overly sympathetic smile, Felix shut the door in Stan's face. "Can't stand that guy."

"You and me both."

"I hope you make partner before him. I don't think I'll be able to stand it if he does."

"He's not a bad lawyer."

"That doesn't make him great."

Vanessa nodded and almost jumped when her phone buzzed. It was a text from Justin.

Why do you want my lawyer's contact info?

Narrowing her eyes, she typed, *So I can tell him where to send me the prenup.*

A moment later, he responded, *Send* YOU *a prenup? Isn't it usually the other way around with the Pryces?*

She sighed. *Don't be dense.* At 25 billion and counting, Justin was worth more than her entire family.

No prenups.

You need to protect yourself.

If I wanted your legal advice, I would've signed a retainer agreement.

She glared at the screen. Felix looked over, his head tilted. "Who's that?"

"A *friend* who's refusing my legal advice."

He snorted. "Not smart. I'd take your advice,

especially if it was free. Does she have any idea how much you bill?"

"I know, right?" Vanessa typed, *Fine. Have it your way. Don't blame me if things go south.*

Go south. As if. A moment later there was another message. *Bring a white dress.*

Stupidly arrogant. But she should've expected that from Barron's heir. Everyone had assumed her parents' prenup was iron-clad...except her mother's lawyer Samantha, shark that she was, had found a way to chip away at it. Now she was questioning the validity of the document in the first place, which was dragging out the horrendous divorce process.

Her phone buzzed again. Vanessa glared at it, then picked it up just in case it was a real client who actually wanted legal advice from her. Instead it was her mother.

I'm finally all moved and settled. There will be a housewarming party on Saturday at six. Bring a date if you can.

Vanessa rolled her neck, trying to relieve the tension. Her mother had been avoiding her and her brothers for the last few weeks, and now came this last-minute notice for an event that was more or less obligatory.

Felix took a big gulp of his coffee. "You okay?"

"Yeah. It's just my mom."

"How's she doing?"

"Great, apparently. She wants to have a house-warming party."

"Oh." He knew—like everyone else in the legal community and Vanessa's social circle—that Ceinlys Pryce was divorcing her husband of almost four decades. "Are you going?"

"I guess. I don't know."

It depended on Justin's plan, which he wasn't telling her.

"I understand your dad's contesting the divorce," Felix said slowly, each word carefully chosen in that lawyerly way of his.

Grunting, she nodded. She didn't know the details of her father's strategy. Her parents weren't talking to her or her brothers about the divorce at all. It hurt her she couldn't talk to her mother about her impending secret wedding and motherhood or her doubts about Justin. Her mother wasn't the best mother—Vanessa knew that much—but it would've been nice to talk things over with someone.

Vanessa sighed and turned her attention to the documents, which had to be finished if she wanted to elope. She had a feeling if she didn't show up at the airport like she was supposed to, Justin would send a platoon of his minions to drag her to wherever he wanted her.

And what a spectacle that would make.

On Tuesday, she bumped into Bobbie, wife of John Highsmith and a partner in her own right, in the break room. A lot of people underestimated her at first glance because she was petite with soft babyish white-gold hair and a pixie face. Nobody who'd ever faced her in a legal battle thought her small and cute though. She was the kind of lawyer Vanessa wanted to be when she grew up: fierce, respected and smart. Not to mention that Bobbie was a straight shooter and never held a grudge. If she hated you, you knew about it. Vanessa, luckily, was on the "like" side.

"Long time no see," Vanessa said.

"Yeah." A bleached smile plumped Bobbie's rosy cheeks as she poured coffee. "How you doing, Vanessa?"

Other than the stress of elopement and a baby? "Oh, fine."

"Good. I heard about your new case with Felix. It's a good one, very important for the firm."

Too bad the client's guilty.

Vanessa's feelings must have shown on her face, because Bobbie gave her a look over the rim of her coffee mug that said *I can eat babies for breakfast if it's billable.* "The kind of thing that can get you noticed if you handle it right."

"I understand. Listen. Um, do you mind if we chat privately?"

The other woman shrugged. "Let's go to my office."

Vanessa grabbed her tea and followed Bobbie to her corner office. The place smelled faintly of paper, leather and old coffee. It was one of the three largest ones on the floor, with the great view of downtown L.A. Stacks of papers, accordion files and legal tomes covered her desk and two tables, while the shelves were occupied by neat rows of leather-bound books. On the desk by her small laptop, she kept a small, framed photo of herself, her husband and their son. They were smiling for the camera, and the boy looked happy. Bobbie was the woman who had it all.

Vanessa closed the door, then took a seat across from the partner.

"So, what's going on?" Bobbie said.

"There's something I've been wondering about." Vanessa wrapped her hands around her cup. "Marriage and motherhood as a female lawyer, you know."

"Are you getting married?" Bobbie's gaze dropped to Vanessa's empty finger.

"No, it's a friend from Stanford." Vanessa cleared her throat. "But it got me thinking. I'm not getting any younger."

Bobbie snorted. "Neither is anybody else. Well, what can I tell you? Husbands aren't too terrible if they understand the demands of our career. So I'd say generally it's best if you get hitched to another lawyer or someone similar. As for a baby, I suppose it's doable, but for a brilliant lawyer with a bright career ahead of her, it can be difficult. Babies are more demanding than any client, and you can't do a damn thing about it. It's not like you can give them back."

Vanessa laughed, and Bobbie smiled.

"Unless you find the lawyer work a cakewalk or you feel some kind of unshakable compulsion to have a child…or your man is okay being a house-husband…I generally advise female attorneys not to do it. It can derail your career. And unfair as it is, child-rearing generally falls on the woman. It's not easy juggling a child and demanding career."

"But you have a son."

"What I had was John's parents. They practically raised the boy. I'm sure you know how it is. You had nannies growing up, didn't you?"

Vanessa nodded. She and her older brothers had had a series of nannies, most of them young. Her mother hadn't kept any of them for long, especially when she suspected they might attract Salazar's attention. Even though Ceinlys knew about his affairs, having it happen under her own roof was just too much.

"They can make things easier. But still, the actual pregnancy and labor and recovery are all on you, and you might resent the fact that the baby's in the way, or that your career's keeping you away from your child. It's not always logical or emotions we're proud of, but it's there. It makes things more complex." Bobbie's smile turned rueful. "Any of that help?"

"Yes." Vanessa nodded. "Thank you."

"Anytime. My door's always open."

As Vanessa left though, she couldn't help but think her situation wouldn't be the way Bobbie had described. Justin knew how her job was. And the baby could have all the best nannies in the world—there was a lot of Sterling money, and knowing Justin and Barron, she doubted they'd be stingy.

But she didn't know where she might fit in. All she had was a sinking feeling that she wouldn't be in the picture for long.

SEVEN

JUSTIN'S JET ARRIVED TO PICK VANESSA UP FROM the small Long Beach airport. Fresh flowers added a nice accent to the luxurious leather and wood-grain interior. He must've had it done specially for the occasion, but she couldn't relax and enjoy it.

Since their texts about the prenup, he hadn't contacted her once. Not that she'd been standing around waiting for something to come through the fax machine. She'd been swamped with work. Solaris Med was an important case, and it was already drawing a lot of media attention with accusations of wrongful termination and sexual harassment flung at the client. It wasn't easy or uplifting to discredit the plaintiff when she knew they were right.

However, she'd managed to draft a fairly good prenup agreement in her very small amounts of spare time. It wasn't her specialty, but she had a few to model from, like her parents' own infamous version. Justin's assets held little appeal, but she wanted a fair custody arrangement for the baby should they divorce.

Or, given what she'd seen in her own family, *when* they divorced.

The jet stopped in Chicago to pick Justin up and then flew on toward god only knew where. She couldn't believe how high-handed and resolute Justin was. On the other hand, what had she expected? This wasn't just any baby.

The heir to the Sterling & Wilson fortune.

Sterling & Wilson was worth billions and had tentacles into the most profitable sectors of six continents. Justin's great-uncle, Barron Sterling, had built it into the massive empire from nothing, and he'd hand-selected Justin to lead the company since he'd been a toddler. Barron and Justin had every important person in the world on speed dial, and there was nothing they couldn't do if they set their minds to it.

It was no wonder Justin had reacted the way he had at the news of her pregnancy. His family tended to be conservative and straight-laced about things. Even if she'd offered to give him the baby no-strings attached, he probably would've insisted on marriage. Then there was Barron's reaction. The man had destroyed people—including some of his own family members—for displeasing him. Vanessa had heard how he'd virtually exiled his own granddaughter Kerri to boarding school for something or other. How would he react if he found out Vanessa wouldn't marry Justin while carrying his child?

She stared at herself in the small window. Her black skirt suit was positively funereal. She'd never wanted to marry. Ever.

Marriage was the most miserable institution in the world, not only for the couple but for their children.

Maybe Justin thought it'd be a good idea to marry, legally speaking. She didn't know much about pregnancy, but she knew there could be serious complications. One of the associates at the firm had gotten pregnant last year, and she had to take six months off due to some problems. As her husband, Justin would have more legal rights in emergency situations, and it made sense he'd want to be in charge of her and their baby just in case.

But after the baby was born, there would be no reason for them to stay together. Couples didn't have to be joined at the hips to raise a child—she knew from experience—and there wasn't even love at the base of their relationship. They could have a clean and simple resolution, with each of them keeping what they'd brought to the marriage. She didn't want a penny of Justin's mon—.

"A penny for your thoughts," Justin said, linking his fingers with hers.

She tried to pull her hand, but he merely tightened his grip. "My billing rate is a little higher than that."

His lips quirked into a smile. "So bill me."

Divorce probably wasn't something they should talk about right now. She combed through possible topics to bring up. "I was wondering if your lawyers know what you're up to."

He sighed. "Are you still worried about the prenup?"

"Aren't you?"

Justin waved his hand. "I'm sure you can draft a simple prenup saying we don't want each other's assets."

"Never trust a lawyer who isn't billing you." She pulled out the prenup she'd drafted. "Here."

"What are you asking for? Half of everything I own?"

She snorted. "I don't want your money. Just a fair custody situation for the child." Her mother had stayed to be with her children. The Pryce prenup was clear: in case of divorce, her mother would not only lose custody, but wouldn't even be able to visit or get in touch with her children until they turned twenty-one.

Then a sudden realization hit her: Ceinlys had stayed way past that point…

For what?

Justin arched an eyebrow. "What about what I might want? Shouldn't you consider some protection as well?"

Vanessa gave herself a good mental shake. This wasn't the time to think about her parents' marriage. "I doubt you're interested in anything I have."

JUSTIN LOOKED OVER AT VANESSA, WHO HAD closed her eyes as if that would block out the world, including him. Maybe she was dreaming about him shoving a prenup in her face.

Her obsession with the agreement amused him. He didn't intend to have one. He didn't want Vanessa to feel that they were less than completely equal in their marriage. If that meant he was being stupid or that he might end up losing half his money, so be it.

Justin watched her softly breathing. It looked like she hadn't slept well in the last few days. The semi-circles under her eyes looked bigger and darker than the week before, and her cheekbones seemed more prominent. He didn't know much about pregnancy, but of course it could be rough on women, especially during the first trimester. And she hadn't told her law firm, so there obviously wouldn't be any accommodation from that end. He made a mental note to take care of it. His wife wasn't going to work herself to death while pregnant. The case she was working on was getting some publicity, which would mean increased pressure to perform.

Vanessa's idea about his not being interested in anything she had contained one glaring blind spot. It was true that none of her material possessions interested him. But he wanted *her*. And not just her, but the life that he knew the two of them could have together.

It astounded him that she didn't believe that was possible. Or maybe it wasn't that incredible, given her background.

To say that her parents didn't have an ideal marriage would be an understatement. A terrible waste since they should've been happy. Salazar must have loved Ceinlys to marry her despite strong opposition from his family, especially his mother, Shirley Pryce. Not even five beautiful grandchildren had been enough to ameliorate her dislike of Ceinlys. Justin didn't understand the old woman's logic; what made it acceptable to love her grandchildren but despise the woman who'd given them to her?

So over the years, Shirley had berated Ceinlys, Salazar had had numerous affairs, and Justin was certain the rumors of Ceinlys's men were true. A situation more or less guaranteed to mess up the children.

Justin didn't want the past to affect what he and Vanessa could have together. They deserved the very best life possible, and he wanted to give it to her, even if it meant hiding their marriage until July against his better judgment. Vanessa seemed worried about her job, but he had no doubt her firm would be understanding of her situation. If not, she could always go someplace else. Hell, he'd buy her a damned law firm if that would make her happy.

If he'd had it his way, everyone would know she was his. They'd be married in a grand ceremony as big as—if not bigger than—the wedding his cousin Kerri had had in Thailand. He would've given her a wedding other women could only dream of.

He rested the knuckle on his left index finger against his lips as he considered. Maybe they could have another ceremony after the baby was born. Something romantic and sentimental, with all their family and friends in attendance… It would be just the thing. Maybe rent out the Ashford Castle in Ireland where they'd had their first vacation together…

The cabin attendant came over. "Sir," she spoke in a low voice. "We'll be landing soon."

He nodded, then glanced over at Vanessa. Her face was lax in sleep.

"That's fine," Justin said, "but we won't be deplaning immediately." He checked the time. "We have about half an hour or so before we need to get going."

"Yes, sir." The cabin attendant slipped away.

Justin pulled out his phone and started typing instructions for his lawyers. Two of the newer associates were coming to join them, but Justin didn't want to discuss what he was about to do with them. Ken Honishi, one of the senior partners at the firm, would be a better choice to take care of the matter.

Vanessa would probably blow a gasket when she found out, but he wanted her to know he was dead serious about this marriage even if she seemed unsure.

Thirty minutes later, he placed a gentle hand on her shoulder. "We need to get going."

Startled, she blinked. "Mm?"

"We're here."

"Oh." She sat up, smoothing her hair. "Sorry. I didn't mean to fall asleep."

"Probably needed the rest." He looked at her belly meaningfully. "Want to get going?"

"Yeah, sure." She got up with care, and they exited the plane together. A gleaming black stretch limo with dark tinted windows waited for them outside.

"You've thought of everything," she said.

"Wanted to make sure you'll be comfortable."

They climbed into the limo. Vanessa settled in the luxurious interior as the driver pulled away from the airport and sighed softly. "So. Are you going to tell me where we are?"

"Canada."

She jerked her head back. “Seriously?”

“We’re about to get married over Niagara Falls.”

Vanessa blinked, unsure if she’d heard him correctly. She’d known they weren’t in Vegas—the air was too moist—but *this?* “There are too many people here. I wasn’t kidding about keeping this quiet.”

“Relax. We’ll be getting married in a helicopter while it’s flying over the falls. I’ve already arranged for it, and a minister’s ready as soon as we pick up the marriage license. There will be only two witnesses—junior associates from a law firm on Sterling & Wilson’s retainer. They won’t talk unless they want to be fired and sued.”

Her lips parted. Justin had been busy, thinking of everything. Sterling & Wilson’s lawyers wouldn’t do anything to jeopardize their retainer.

“This is the best I could arrange on short notice. I know it’s nobody’s dream wedding, but we can have a real, grand ceremony later after the baby.” He pulled out a dark navy box and took her left hand. Inside the box was a diamond ring. The simple platinum setting showed off the size and superior cut and clarity of the stone surrounded by smaller sapphires the exact color of her eyes. “For the engagement. I wanted to get something custom designed, but there wasn't enough time."

"It's perfect," she whispered as a sudden lump formed in her throat.

He put the ring on her finger and kissed her knuckles. The sparkling gem made it seem so much more real. She was really getting married.

Her mother had a similar piece in her jewelry box, although the stone types were reversed—a huge sapphire in the center surrounded by small diamonds. It was her engagement ring, which she hadn't worn in ages. Vanessa knew her father had proposed in the most romantic setting he could manage and professed undying love. She'd seen his letters.

My love for you will never die. So long as you love me, we'll be happy and together till death do us part. Ceinlys, I know you're worried about my mother's reaction, but it isn't her life, it's ours. Will you take a chance? I'll make you the happiest woman in the world forever and ever.

"Vanessa?"

She jerked her chin up and looked at Justin's frowning face. "Sorry. I sort of zoned out."

Justin's frown melted into an ironically skewed smile. "Is the rock disappointing?"

She smacked his arm. "No! It's so big, it's almost vulgar."

"I was going to get a four-carat stone, but I thought it would look wrong on you." He traced her ring finger. "Your hands are so delicate…you need something simple, elegant and graceful."

She licked her lower lip. His words seeped all the way to her bones in syrupy sweetness, and her mind shivered with longing and a sliver of fear.

"Vanessa… I swear to you, I'll make you happy…as happy as I know you're going to make me," he said.

His gaze was absolutely steady. He wasn't just talking, carried by the moment. Cold sweat filmed her palms and the back of her neck. Hadn't Ceinlys often spoken of the madness of deriving happiness from others, how Salazar had let her down? That could easily be Vanessa's future too. Justin had all the things that had made Salazar irresistible to women: a charming personality, looks, money and power.

And all the beauties who used to grace his arms wouldn't give up just because he was married. Just look at all those women throwing themselves at Salazar. How could Justin's situation be any different? Vanessa would be one of many stars that orbited around him, while he was the center of her universe. Panic balled in her gut.

"Vanessa?" Justin prompted.

"Yes?"

"You're zoning out again."

"Sorry. I was just wondering…" She took a deep breath, then held the air in her lungs so she wouldn't start hyperventilating. "How long were you planning to be in Toronto? I need to go back to L.A. on Saturday."

"Didn't block out any time for a honeymoon?"

Cringing, she shook her head. "It's not like we can have one. Our marriage is secret, remember?"

"That sounds so clandestine." He gave her a meaningful look. "*Secret* Wife."

She looked away as her heart squeezed. What a ridiculous reaction. She wasn't thrilled at being called "wife," secret or otherwise. This was temporary, and she was *not* going to end up like her mother.

Because she looked so much like her mother, most people thought she'd marry well and have everything catered to her. Except she knew better. Her grandmother had often lamented about how poisonous and ephemeral her mother's looks were.

"If Ceinlys had been just slightly less beautiful she would never have been able to marry Salazar. Mark my words, as she grows older, her hold on him will weaken. Fading youth can never keep a man's heart. One day he'll wake up and wonder what he ever saw in her. And she'll be sorry. But by then it will be too late." She raised a wrinkled but absolutely steady finger. "This is why you look at the pedigree. The character. You never marry a woman solely for her beauty."

Vanessa pushed aside her grandmother's conversation. Shirley Pryce hadn't limited herself to just her sister's ears. Vanessa also knew how disappointed Shirley was that she looked so much like Ceinlys.

"If only you'd gotten the Pryce eyes or nose..." Shirley had sighed, searching Vanessa's face. "If you'd been a boy, at least you could've had the Pryce profile. Ah well, at least you're pretty. Good men will marry you for that...assuming you don't over-educate yourself."

Vanessa snuffed the memory and concentrated on the present. "Mom's having a housewarming party on Saturday," she said to Justin, "and she wants me there. I couldn't beg off, especially with all my brothers coming." Short notice or no, they'd wanted to attend. "Well, except for Shane, of course."

Justin frowned. "Where is Shane anyway? I haven't seen him in months."

"You or anyone else. He went to South Africa in May, but since then...nada." She shook her head. "He's never pulled something like this. Dad's thinking about sending men out there to drag him back to L.A."

"That's pretty high-handed."

"I know. Shocking, given that it's Dad." Vanessa snorted. "But in this case, I actually agree with the idea."

Justin shrugged. "Well let me know if I can help. In the meantime, if you want, we can get married today, then fly out to L.A. together tomorrow. I want to see how Ceinlys is doing."

"But—"

"Don't give yourself an aneurism, okay? She invited me too."

Vanessa's eyes widened. "She did?"

"Yeah. She apparently heard something about my relocating to California."

"Justin! I thought you were staying in Chicago."

"Why would I do that when my wife and child are going to be in California?" He gave her a small, smile. "Don't worry. She won't have any idea. I'm going to be in San Francisco. I even rented a corporate condo, not that I plan to actually live there."

"Where are you going to be?"

"In L.A. With you."

"Everyone's going to know then."

"Leave it to me to keep it quiet," Justin said, his tone absolutely unshakable. "I can be very discreet."

EIGHT

It took no time at all to get the marriage license. The clerk looked only politely interested as she processed the paperwork and gave them their document. "Here you go. Congratulations." Her tone indicated it was the fiftieth time she'd said it that day. Vanessa was just relieved she didn't seem to connect the dots.

She and Justin went to their hotel afterward to freshen up before the actual ceremony. Justin had booked a sumptuously decorated suite overlooking the Falls.

Since she didn't want to draw any attention, she'd brought a lacy white cocktail dress with matching shoes and the pearls she'd inherited from her grandmother. Justin put on a tux with a white tie, while she commandeered the vanity to touch up her makeup and hair.

She kept her hand steady as she applied a thin coat of lipstick. It felt so surreal to think that soon she'd be a missus. She pressed her palm against her still flat belly. At least Justin hadn't accused her of lying about her pregnancy or denying that it could be his child. He'd treated her right, and the least she could do was return the favor.

So long as they were married…so long as he was faithful, she'd be a good wife.

"Hey, you look beautiful," Justin said from the doorway. One arm was held behind his back. He walked over, sweeping the arm out with a magician's flourish and producing a large plumeria blossom. "Here." He put it carefully into her hair. "Your favorite."

Something she couldn't quite identify welled in her chest, and it felt like her ribcage would snap. "Where did you get it?" Her voice shook slightly despite her best effort.

"Concierge." He gave her a quick kiss on the mouth, careful not to smear the lipstick. "We have to get going now."

She draped a long black coat over her shoulders and left the suite with Justin. Their limo took them to a helipad not too far from their hotel, where a helicopter was waiting. The setting sun streaked the sky with orange, gold and purples, and the shining white finish on the helicopter reflected the warm colors.

A young woman in a pink dress came over with a bouquet made with fresh tropical flowers and white roses. The plumerias matched the one in Vanessa's hair, and the florist placed a boutonnière on Justin's tux.

Four men stood outside and said hello at the sight of Justin and Vanessa. The oldest was in his mid- to late forties, his face round and plump with laugh lines forking out from the corners of his eyes. He wore a cheap but well-fitting suit, and his receding hair was slicked back from his face, making his forehead look exceptionally large.

The second oldest was probably in his early forties, his face weathered and uneven like avocado skin. He wore a suit that was a size too small, and thick blue veins covered the back of his hands like spider webs. He snapped a few photos with a huge black camera.

The other two were younger, in their mid-twenties. Their suits were identical—dark and expensive but not necessarily better fitting than the older man's. They carried well-cared-for briefcases. Their expressions were relaxed, but something about them told Vanessa they didn't smile much. She knew without asking that they were the lawyers Justin had been talking about.

The oldest man introduced himself as Aaron, and turned out to be the minister. "You make a beautiful couple."

"Thank you, sir."

The other two handed out business cards embossed with their firm's name. She put them in her coat pocket and climbed into the helicopter with Justin's help.

The interior was all cream leather with tropical blossoms and pale pink and white ribbons. The walls were lined with padded panels. The air smelled of sweet flowers and powdered sugar.

Aaron and the photographer took a seat facing Justin. She slowly lowered herself next to Justin and consciously relaxed each of her muscles. The lawyers sat behind them. The door shut when everyone was settled, and the pilot started the engine.

The helicopter was much quieter than Vanessa had expected, better soundproofed even than her father's helicopter.

The sound system played Wagner's "Here Comes the Bride" as they flew over the falls. The dark water churned and foamed underneath. Water drops spread out in a white mist and split the sun into rainbow arcs.

After some time to appreciate the scenery, the music faded and Aaron started the ceremony. His voice was surprisingly resonant and carried clearly over the muffled sound of the blades chopping the air. He didn't drag out the ceremony with a flowery speech about true love and commitment, which relieved Vanessa—this had nothing to do with love—but he didn't seem to rush things, either.

As a hammer beat inside her head, she focused on the majestic natural surroundings and drawing air into her lungs in a steady rhythm. *This isn't permanent.* It was just for the baby. She wasn't like her mother. She didn't need a husband to afford a decent lifestyle. She could opt out at any time and still create an excellent life for herself and her baby.

There was simply no reason to worry about the marriage or her future.

She blinked when Justin poked her gently on the side. She glanced at the minister and blushed. "I do," she said, hoping that was the right answer.

He beamed at her and moved on to the next part of the ceremony.

Relieved, she let out a soft sigh and slumped in her seat until the minister ordered them to exchange rings. He held a pair of simple platinum bands.

Her hands grew clammy and started shaking.

Justin squeezed them and kept his eyes on hers. "I give you this ring as a symbol of my commitment to you. Know that from now on, all that I am, all that I have are yours." He slid the band on her finger. "Wear it with happiness and think of my vow to you."

Her mouth dried. She hadn't prepared a vow. She'd been so busy working and trying not to think about their elopement. One would think she should be able to extemporaneously come up with something clever, given her experience and education. She was one of the best lawyers in the state!

But the only thing her hormone-addled and sleep-deprived brain could come up with was, "With this ring, I thee wed." So she murmured the six words and put the ring on his finger.

"I now pronounce you husband and wife."

The joyous tune of Mendelssohn's "Wedding March" burst from the helicopter's sound system. Aaron and the lawyers clapped, while the photographer snapped more shots.

Justin linked their left hands together and kissed her. Her mouth parted like it couldn't wait. Maybe it was something in the state of her mind that made her want to cling to him. What had just happened felt like a scene from some surrealist's imagination, and Justin was the only thing that felt normal and sane in a world where the clocks were melting.

Before she could prolong and deepen the kiss, Justin pulled back. A bemused smile ghosted on his face. "Wife."

Because it was the right thing to say, she murmured, "Husband."

Her stomach jittered, and she managed to smile while locking her jaw. Even if it wasn't something she'd ever wanted, she wasn't going to throw up at her wedding ceremony.

"Is there anything else planned for the evening?" Vanessa asked, as their limo glided toward their hotel.

Justin nodded. "We have a dinner reservation."

"Okay."

He frowned. She seemed listless and her voice lacked its usual vigor. On the other hand, she hadn't been herself all day. She'd been so tense, her skin cool and clammy. He'd chalked it up to her uncertainty about their marriage. But now it seemed like it was more. When Vanessa sighed, Justin looked at her more closely in the dying light. Tension marked her lips, and her eyes seemed to have sunken deeper into her skull. There was something wilted about the way she slumped in the seat and let her head loll.

"Are you okay?" he asked.

"I'm fine." She smiled, but it didn't reach her eyes. "Besides, I have to eat. Right?" She patted her belly.

Justin cursed himself. Knowing her, she'd probably half-killed herself to finish up all her work to take the day off. A lot of people thought she wouldn't take her career seriously, given how wealthy her family was and the big trust that she inherited when she'd graduated from college, but she worked harder than anyone he knew.

"We can always get room service," he said. "It's no big deal."

Relief flashed through her eyes. "You don't mind?"

"Nope. We can go next time. Let me cancel it." He texted his assistant, telling her to cancel everything booked after the wedding ceremony.

"Thank you."

"You're my wife. You come first."

She nodded, but she broke eye contact. Her face seemed frozen in disbelief and wistful resignation. She was probably preoccupied with all sorts of thoughts, most likely about what this marriage meant to the two of them, what sort of family they would create together. With the Sterlings, it was Barron at the center of all sorts of rollercoaster dramas. He could be delicate when he had to, but in general he had the finesse of a bull in Pamplona. With the Pryces, it was Salazar, Ceinlys and Dane, the oldest of Vanessa's four brothers. Salazar had cheated on his wife ever since Justin could remember. Because of the prenup, Salazar had been brazen about his other women. Justin was certain Ceinlys had had her share of lovers. He'd heard hushed whispers, and he didn't blame her one bit for wanting some affection while her husband flaunted his mistresses.

Justin wondered what it would've been like to grow up with parents like that. His parents certainly hadn't been perfect, but they'd been deeply committed to each other. His father would've considered it dishonorable to break his wedding vows.

The limo pulled up in front of their hotel, and a smartly uniformed man opened the door. Justin climbed out and extended his hand, helping Vanessa out. She swayed a bit on her feet. "Sure you're okay?" he asked.

"I'm fine." She gave him a wan smile. "Just hungry."

Justin nodded and took her to their suite, keeping a hand at the small of her back. She seemed more fragile, like she'd lost weight. "Are you having morning sickness?" he asked when they were in their suite.

"No. I can't eat a lot, but I'm not nauseous or anything." She sat on the love seat, her whole body sagging in relief. She stretched out her legs. "What are you in the mood for?"

"I'm pretty simple. Meat and potatoes should do it. How about you?"

"Maybe…some lightly prepared fish, if they have any? Nothing too heavy."

Justin picked up the room service menu and glanced at it. They had salmon in a tarragon cream sauce, but it was probably not what she wanted. He didn't know if the kitchen had anybody who could make decent seafood. Vanessa was undoubtedly spoiled by her brother's chefs. He dialed and placed their order, instructing them to prepare Vanessa's fish lightly without the cream sauce. He added an order for extra bread and hung up.

"That was a pretty picky order."

He sat next to her. "So? It's their job to make you happy."

Wordlessly, she rested her head on his shoulder, and he put an arm around her. Peace settled over him. He'd been on the edge ever since Vanessa had left Chicago the week before. Even though she'd agreed to the marriage, he hadn't been completely sure she'd show up on Friday. Over the ten years they'd spent together, she'd been fickle in her affections, changing her mind frequently about their relationship.

But now she was officially his.

SOME TIME LATER THEIR ROOM SERVICE ARRIVED. Justin got up to sign for it, and Vanessa sighed, missing him next to her. The server disappeared, and she moved over to the table to have dinner. She wasn't that hungry, but she knew she had to eat for the sake of the baby growing in her womb.

The table was beautifully set with two red roses in the center. She picked one up and inhaled. It smelled fresh and dewy.

Then she suddenly stopped, feeling Justin's gaze on her. She raised an eyebrow, but he merely gave her a devilish smile.

They sat at the table. Justin had ordered a steak for himself. He looked at her salmon and asked, "Let me know if you don't like it."

She took a bite of the firm orange flesh. It was moist…and perfectly seasoned and prepared. "Mm. Good." She smiled, her fingers toying with a glass of mineral water. "It's so weird to eat without any wine." Unless she was working, she always had a glass of wine. "You should've ordered some champagne."

"Let's wait until the baby's born. Then we can enjoy it together."

Her smile faltered. It seemed unreal, both to think about the baby's birth and the idea that Justin would be with her till then, and that he would want to drink champagne with her. That was a long time to be committed to a woman. She'd seen some associates at her firm who'd gotten huge during pregnancy. Would he still find her attractive? Or would he want somebody who didn't waddle?

If one of her friends had been having the kind of doubts she was having, she would've told her that any man who didn't worship the body of the woman who was pregnant with his child was a worthless jackass. But she couldn't seem to muster the same certainty for herself. *What a hypocrite*, she thought.

She made a mental note to talk with Mark's fiancée, Hilary Rosenberg. Out of all the women close to her, Hilary was the one who would know what Vanessa was going through the best.

"So. Living arrangements," Vanessa said as she broke off a decent-sized chunk of fish with her fork. "Where do you exactly plan to live in L.A.? Have you found a rental?"

"Nope. I plan to stay at your place."

"Justin… People are going to notice and talk."

"I doubt it. I checked out your building already. It's mostly occupied by young professionals. Lawyers, doctors, consultants and so on."

"You checked it out." She had an image of him lying on the roof of the building across the street, with a telephoto lens and access to a private detective. "Okay, so what if you did?"

"When was the last time any of your neighbors said hello to you?"

She thought back. "I don't know. Maybe a few days ago when I ran into Sarah?"

"Uh huh. And how often do you run into someone?"

"Not that often," she admitted. Being a young professional meant long hours. When she'd moved in, probably half a month had gone by before she'd met anyone in the building.

"Right. So, no real issue. And if anybody sees me at the airport or anything, they'll just assume I'm in L.A. on business. But I doubt it'll be a problem. L.A. isn't interested in me. Too preoccupied with Hollywood."

That was true enough. The media had better stories to chase.

"Don't look so serious. Besides, if you want a pregnancy buddy—do women have those?—you can always ping Kerri. She's expecting, too."

"Really? I had no idea." Vanessa had been to Kerri's wedding at Barron's invitation. The Sterlings were family friends, but she'd never been overly close to Barron's granddaughter. They lived too far apart, and Kerri had been out of the country for most of her life. But now they were cousins by marriage.

"Barron told me last week. You two are at about the same stage, too. I think she's six or seven weeks along now. If her kid's anything like her, it's going to drive her insane." He smiled as he dragged his knife through the meat. "Don't worry. I was a complete angel."

"That remains to be seen." Vanessa ripped a small piece of bread. "Do you ever think about your future, like ten years down the road?"

"Nope."

"Why not?" She'd assumed he thought about his future all the time. He was one of the few who had everything he could hope for. Why *not* think about it?

"Because nobody knows what's going to happen ten years from now. But I don't let the uncertain future take away the certain happiness of today."

And that inexplicably touched her. The day had been beautiful, thanks to Justin. He'd done so much to make it special even though they were eloping on short notice. It embarrassed her she hadn't prepared anything. She couldn't even blame her work since Justin was just as busy as she was.

After they finished dinner, Justin led her over and opened the door to the adjoining bedroom. Vanessa gasped at the scented candles flickering everywhere in the room. They cast a romantic glow, and she felt herself start to melt. "You've thought of everything."

He hugged her from behind. "It's our wedding night. I wanted it to be special."

"It's already special." She blinked away the sudden moisture gathering in her eyes. She didn't know why she felt so weepy all of a sudden. This was such a sweet gesture.

If you're not careful, you're going to fall in love with him.

And she didn't want that at all. Nothing was more seductive and dangerous than the belief that love conquered all. The reality was that love could lose out to an awful lot of quotidian circumstances. Couples broke up over money, although she knew money wouldn't be an issue in their marriage. But there would be other things. There were always other things.

Justin buried his face in the crook of her neck. "You smell like heaven. I can't believe you're finally mine."

Her heart thumped. She swallowed and turned around. She wasn't the only one who "belonged" now. He was hers.

She thought about the effort he'd put into making the day as perfect as possible for her. She couldn't be like him and only focus on the happiness of the present, but she didn't have to let the worries about their future ruin the moment. The least she could do was appreciate it and make the night as memorable as possible for both of them.

She put a hand to his cheek; the stubble scraped her skin. Cradling the back of his head, she pulled him down for a kiss.

His firm, sexy mouth slanted over hers. She swallowed a gasp at the possessive way his large hand traveled under her skirt and cupped her butt. It certainly wasn't the first time they'd made love—they were intimately familiar with each other's bodies—but this was the first time she felt like he was really making his stake clear.

A small knot of fear unfurled.

His tongue ran over the seam of her mouth, skittering her anxiety, then it probed gently, seeking an entry. Grateful he was pushing away her doubts, she pulled it into her mouth and rubbed her tongue against it, sucking it. She could feel the beginning of a moan vibrate in his chest, and her nipples beaded almost painfully. They were ultra-sensitive now that she was pregnant.

He unzipped her dress. His eyes filled with glittering desire and reverence as the silk whispered down her body, revealing creamy skin. The bra and thong she wore were bridal white, delicate with lace. She flushed, suddenly shy. This was...different from all the previous times. This was a step toward their entwined lives.

"You look divine," he murmured. His lips traced every slope and curve of her exposed body, and warmth pooled in her core, making her slick and needy.

His eyes on hers, he took off his clothes. He was gorgeous, his sculpted, powerful chest dusted with crisp hair that followed his tight, ridged belly to the junction of his muscular thighs. Vanessa licked her lips. Again, this felt different—like this was their first time.

He deposited her on the bed and covered her body with his. Their hands linked, and he kissed her again, deeply and hungrily. She kissed him back, unable to help herself. His hard, thick length settled against her wet folds, and as he rocked, his chest brushed against the pointed peaks of her nipples, sending electric shocks of pleasure along her spine.

Their breaths mingled, and she was unable to look away as he slipped inside her, filling and stretching her. Her inner muscles clamped down on him, needing more. Despite his hungry kiss earlier, his thrusts were measured and steady, as though he knew exactly what to do to drive her insane. Pleasure built, at first slowly and steadily, but then it seemed to gain a momentum of its own, growing bigger, faster…all consuming.

The pleasure was drowning her, but unlike before, she couldn't break free, keep control of any part of herself. It was Justin—his scent, his sound, his warmth, the knowledge of his vow—that pulled her deeper and deeper. Even as the orgasm shot through her with a blinding intensity, she drowned in him.

And when he joined her, his voice hoarse as he cried out, they drowned together, their limbs tangled. And she was afraid she might never reemerge.

NINE

VANESSA OPENED HER EYES. THE ROOM WAS dark but warm, and she was alone in bed. Had the wedding been a dream? No. She was in a hotel room, and her body was pleasantly sore from loving the night before.

She turned and saw a bedside clock glow: ten thirty-three. She wondered briefly if it was p.m. still, then bolted upright and covered her mouth as nausea hit her. Clenching her teeth, she ran to the connecting bathroom. She managed to reach the toilet before she lost everything in her stomach.

Feeling wrought out and gross, she slumped. The toilet flushed, and a big hand rubbed her back.

She closed her eyes. Of all the things for Justin to witness. "Help me up." Her legs felt like wet noodles.

He pulled her up easily, and led her to the sink as though he'd read her mind.

"Can I have a few minutes in private?" she asked.

"Sure. I'll be right outside if you want anything."

She nodded, but she wouldn't be needing him again. There was nothing in her stomach now. Sighing she rubbed her face. She didn't know why her body decided to start having morning sickness all of a sudden. Maybe it was the strange city and bed. Once she went home, she'd feel better.

After brushing her teeth, she took a quick shower. Morning sickness or no, the hot water cleared her head, and a good night's sleep had put a lot of things into clearer perspective. She would talk with Hilary as soon as she could, but at the same time she wouldn't be so gloomy about the marriage. What was done was done. Hadn't she known that becoming pregnant with Justin's child would bring about changes to her life? She couldn't deny either Justin or the child a chance to bond with each other. They had the right, and she had a feeling Justin would be a good father.

She put on the hotel robe and went out with a towel wrapped around her hair. Justin was at a desk, working on his laptop.

"Anything urgent?" she asked.

"No. You want to eat? I already had something, but didn't order any for you because I wasn't sure what you might be in the mood for."

Ugh. Food. "How about… some hot lemon tea and dry toast. Maybe with some fruit?"

Justin ordered while she dried her hair. She could hear his voice over the whirring of the dryer. Her toes curled at the deep, masculine tone. He hadn't been cold to her after he'd found out she was pregnant. It was like some switch inside him had been flipped. Maybe there was another switch inside him that could make him permanently faithful, sweet and perfect.

When her hair was dry and falling in sleek layers around her face and shoulders, she went outside without bothering to pull it up. It seemed like too much work.

The breakfast was waiting. Justin had also ordered a pitcher of freshly squeezed orange juice. "Just in case." He kissed her. "Take your time. Our flight doesn't need to leave until noon anyway to make your mother's party."

Vanessa snapped her fingers. "I knew I was forgetting something. I have to buy her a present."

"Don't worry. I'll take care of it."

"Really? What are you planning to get in my name?"

"A high-end espresso machine. Ceinlys likes her coffee."

Her eyes widened. "You noticed?"

"Of course." He tapped the tip of her nose. "I notice a lot more than people think I do."

She frowned and nibbled on her toast. Justin had met her mother maybe five times.

"Don't worry. Everything I notice about you is positive," he said, his voice light.

Wasn't that positive back in November. But she didn't want to bring up their fight. "I'm glad. And I see I need to perfect my poker face."

"I like it better when you're open."

"I'm a *lawyer*. I can't have everyone reading me like that."

"It's not everyone. Just me."

JUSTIN DIDN'T KNOW EXACTLY HOW TO EXPLAIN IT, but he knew nobody else understood Vanessa the way he did. It was crazy how he could just look at her face—no matter how impassive—and perceive her feelings. Just moments ago, when her guard was down…he could almost read her thoughts. And he liked it that he could understand what his wife needed without her having to say it.

He hadn't been kidding about making her happy. His vow had been one hundred percent in earnest. He was dead serious about his commitment to their marriage, and he knew it could work great given how compatible they were, sexually and otherwise.

His own parents had gotten married because his mother had been pregnant. They grew to love each other in a quiet, calm way and had an amazing marriage that lasted until his father had passed away. Justin didn't believe in over-the-top emotional love being an essential part of a relationship.

Love like that was irrational, uncontrollable and impulsive. It also produced too much influence; all he had to do was look at his cousin Kerri's parents to know why that kind of love was a terrible idea. When Kerri's father had died, her mother had lost it. Not even Barron's money and connections could fix whatever had broken inside her, and she hadn't been able to look at her own daughter with affection after that.

Justin wasn't going to let anything weaken him like that. He had responsibilities, and the only way he could manage them well was with a cool, rational mind.

So was it the cool, rational part of your mind that helped you fuck Vanessa last night?

Justin forced the thought aside. He hated it when his subconscious tried to overanalyze his personal life.

VANESSA ARRIVED AT THE HOUSEWARMING PARTY alone, with Justin scheduled to show up anywhere from half an hour to an hour later. Ceinlys's new place was on the top floor of a condo complex equidistant from her three children's homes. Currently

Shane didn't live in the city, and Dane might as well not have had a place either, given how rarely he occupied his penthouse.

The sound system played Debussy, her mother's favorite composer. The place was sparsely but elegantly appointed with comfortable cream and champagne couches and soft rugs over hardwood flooring. A few expensively framed photos of Vanessa and her brothers sat on the shelves. There was no sign of Salazar anywhere.

Her brothers Iain and Mark were already there with their fiancées Jane and Hilary. Iain and Mark both had the classic profile the Pryce men were famous for. Jane and Hilary glowed, and Vanessa felt sort of guilty about getting married before Mark and Hilary. They'd set their date for a June wedding. At least she wouldn't be stealing their thunder since she and Justin would keep their wedding quiet until July.

She greeted everyone, and her mother emerged from the open kitchen.

Ceinlys was in a chic Chanel dark blue dress that stopped half an inch above her knees. Her glossy hair was twisted into an elegant bun, and a sapphire hairpiece glittered under the recessed lights. She hugged Vanessa. "I wasn't sure if you could come, what with your firm working you half to death."

"I wouldn't miss it for the world."

"Good, good." She peered at Vanessa. "Have you lost weight? You look so tired."

"I'm fine." Vanessa wasn't telling her mother she was pregnant. "Nothing a few good nights' sleep won't cure."

"See that you get some sleep tonight then."

There was another arrival, and Ceinlys went to meet them.

It looked like her mother had invited everyone in their social circle. The place became packed with people both young and old, every one of them dressed to be seen and admired. Maybe they were privy to something Vanessa wasn't, because as far as she knew, her mother had a horrible prenup that left her with nothing. Or maybe they wanted to see how the female half of The Eternal Couple was doing. So many had assumed it would be Salazar leaving Ceinlys, not the other way around.

"They're probably wondering when her boyfriend's going to show up," Iain muttered from behind her.

"You're such a cynic," Vanessa said.

"I actually agree with him," Mark said. "They're probably wondering who she'll marry once she gets rid of Dad."

"You two are awful. Where are Hilary and Jane?"

"Making themselves scarce," Iain said.

Sure enough, they had vanished. They were never sure how Ceinlys would receive them.

"But this isn't as bad as I thought."

"What do you mean?"

Mark grew thoughtful. "At least nobody's shunning her. They're treating her like a genuine friend. I think she could use a few right now."

Shame dampened Vanessa's mood. She'd been too worried about her mother's prenup to ask how she was doing. No, it had been worse than that. She'd questioned her mother numerous times about the divorce, whether or not she'd thought it through. And that wasn't what her mother needed. "You think she's happier?"

"Who knows? She's not talking about it, but I think she's doing better than before. Don't you?"

Iain finished his wine. "Anything has to be better. I don't think Dad made her very happy."

"Do you think he ever truly loved her?" Vanessa asked before she could bite her tongue.

Her brothers stared at her like she'd grown a third breast…between her eyes. "No. Never," Iain said. "He probably married Mom because she was the best-looking woman he could find."

Mark nodded.

Vanessa said nothing as she watched her mother hug a friend. Salazar must have loved Ceinlys at some point. She didn't know what had killed that love. She never got the sense that their feelings had merely cooled with time. If so, they could've at least been polite and considerate. But there was always a subtle undercurrent of meanness to what her father and mother did and said, like they wanted to hurt each other.

The back of her neck prickled, and Iain whistled. "Hey, Justin's here."

"Huh," Mark said. "Maybe that explains it.

"What?" Vanessa said.

"Mom invited London Bickham, but she declined. Maybe she said she couldn't because she knew he would be here. Awkward."

Vanessa cringed, then let out a relieved sigh. It would've been more than awkward to face London here. If she hadn't told Justin about her pregnancy, he'd still be with her. Vanessa pushed away a flash of hot jealousy at the thought.

"Not that I ever thought they'd last as a couple. London's a little…bland," Mark said.

A dry laugh came from behind them. It was their oldest brother, Dane. "Is that the new euphemism for brainless?" He was in a rumpled dress shirt with the sleeves rolled up to his elbows. He was a carbon copy of their father, with classic features and cool gray eyes, but he had none of Salazar's charm. Nobody knew where he'd inherited his abrasive personality.

Mark's mouth turned into a flat slit. "She's a family friend, Dane. You don't have to be so nasty."

"Truth is painful, not nasty." Dane glanced at Vanessa. "I've been hearing rumors, baby sister.

You're going to make partner for sure if you can prove Solaris Med is"—a cynical smile lifted a corner of his mouth—"innocent."

Grinding her teeth, Vanessa reined in her temper. It killed her that she had to defend a client who was unquestionably guilty. She might be their counsel, but she had her standards.

"Of course you wouldn't be required to do that if you'd climbed the ladder of family connections." Before she could snap at him, he turned to Iain and Mark. "So how come Shane's not here?"

Iain shrugged. "Tried contacting him a few times, but he never responded."

"Whatever's in South Africa must be damned interesting," Vanessa muttered as a pang of envy reverberated through her. She wished she could just disappear for months and months too.

"He's not in South Africa," Dane said. "I checked. He's in Morocco."

Vanessa felt her jaw drop. "Doing what?"

Dane shrugged. "Don't know, but I should bring him home. It's only fair he suffer with the rest of us through this."

Then in her peripheral vision, she noticed Justin laughing at something a slim blonde had said. Vanessa couldn't tell exactly who the woman was—she had her back to Vanessa—but her well-fitted dress showed off lovely curves and a tight butt. And unlike Vanessa, the blonde was tall with seemingly endless legs.

"Did Mom invite a lawyer?" Mark asked. "You look like you just spotted an enemy."

"No." She forced a smile. "Just thinking about something. Excuse me. I'm going to go snag a drink."

Vanessa made her way around the room, trying to get a look at the blonde without being obvious. The woman was gorgeous in front too. *Maybe she's an aspiring actress or something*. L.A. was filthy with them.

When the woman laid a hand on Justin's sleeve, Vanessa ground her teeth. She wanted to slap the bitch, but she and Justin were trying to keep their marriage secret. Nothing would get them outed faster than public jealousy.

Still, Justin didn't have to look quite so happy while flirting with the woman!

Vanessa poured herself a glass of ginger ale and stuffed her mouth with a miniature appetizer, wishing she could leave.

Justin looked around. He swore he'd seen Vanessa chatting with her brothers, but now she was gone.

He sighed impatiently. Once it got around that Justin Sterling was in the room, everyone wanted to talk to him. A few people asked how he knew Ceinlys, like they wanted to figure out how they might be able to use their connection to her to suck up to him. Even so, he smiled at everyone politely and laughed at the appropriate moments. Unlike Barron, he didn't believe in baring his talons…until he had to gut somebody. His great-uncle thought everyone should fear him. Justin reserved that for those who worked for him or who dared to cross him.

Finally he found Vanessa in the kitchen corner, hidden from everyone. She had a tray of finger food and cubed cheese.

"Ah ha! So you got all the good stuff," he said.

"Not really. What are you doing here?"

"Looking for you." He popped a cheddar block into his mouth. "This is great cheese."

"I'm glad you approve." Her voice crackled with fight. "I had nothing to do with it."

He frowned. "You angry with me for some reason?"

"No." She didn't meet his gaze, and immediately started drinking her ginger ale.

He narrowed his eyes. "You know, you're supposed to be honest with me. Wife."

"Shh!"

"Tell me, or I'm going to keep using the W-word."

"Fine. I don't like your shirt."

"There's nothing wrong with my shirt!"

"There is now."

Her face set in a mutinous line, and he laughed. "Fine, fine. I'll get out of it. Tonight." He abruptly stopped laughing. "Now, tell me what's wrong."

Sighing, she sagged. "I just don't feel well." She looked down at her belly meaningfully. "But I'm going out to mingle. So why don't you try to do the same?"

Justin watched her leave, but she didn't fool him. She was upset about something, even if she didn't want to tell him. Sighing, he rubbed the back of his neck.

"Justin! There you are."

He pasted on a smile for Ceinlys and gave her a tight hug. "You look good."

"Always the flatterer. Thank you *so* much for coming. I wasn't sure if you could."

"I can always make time for you," he said. Even though he couldn't tell her yet, she was his mother-in-law and Vanessa was fond of her. That meant she was important to him as well.

"The painting arrived today. It's gorgeous. Thank you."

"My pleasure." He didn't tell her Barron's new art curator, Catherine Fairchild, had selected the piece. Catherine was engaged to Blaine Davis, who was Salazar's child by another woman. Justin didn't think it prudent to mention the fact.

"More than a few guests have been asking to meet you, but if you like, I can arrange things to avoid all the introductions. I know it can be tedious," Ceinlys said.

"Thanks, but that won't be necessary." She could probably maneuver things to ensure he wouldn't be bothered. She was an exceptional hostess from years of trying to live up to the exacting Pryce standards. But it wasn't like he could hang out with Vanessa at the party, and he didn't want to stand around in a corner by himself all evening long.

"Well, then." Ceinlys looped her arm through his. "Shall we?"

Peggy Teeter scowled as Stan lit his cigarette in their bedroom. It was technically his bedroom, but she thought of it as "theirs" since she was sleeping there too. "I told you, no smoking in the house."

"Just one."

"No." She glared at him. "I mean it."

"It's a stress reliever."

"We just had sex! If you need more stress relief, go exercise."

"Why are you so weird about it?"

She pressed her lips together. An associate at a law firm, Stan liked to argue and could negotiate his way out of almost anything. For once she wished she'd never met him, not even to pump him for information. "My mom has lung cancer."

That shut Stan up. He stubbed out the cigarette. "Sorry."

"Not your fault. Just don't smoke again in the house." She cleared her throat. "What's got you so upset anyway?"

"It's one of the associates at the firm. I told you already. Vanessa Pryce."

Peggy's heart thumped oddly at the mention of the name. "What about her?"

"She's been taking too much personal time off. It's such bullshit. And you know what? There are rumors that she's going to make partner this July."

"I thought you were next."

He shook his head. "I don't know the right people, not the way she does anyway. The firm only cares about how much business you can pull in, and they think she can do it."

"Aren't you a better lawyer than her?"

"Yeah." He shrugged. "But she's not bad. At the end of the day, that's all that matters—be good enough and bring in the business."

"Doesn't she have to buy a stake in the firm?"

"Not an issue for somebody like her. She can just tap her trust fund or something."

Peggy nodded, only half-listening to Stan's complaints about Vanessa. The woman seemed loaded, but then her family was rich. Lung cancer treatment was expensive, and Peggy had done everything she could to finance it. But now she was out of options, and Vanessa seemed like a perfect person to help.

She just needed to find a good approach.

TEN

VANESSA HAD STAYED BEHIND AT HER MOTHER's place to help clean up, and Justin slipped into her condo with the spare key she'd given him on the flight from Canada. The party had gone spectacularly well, with Ceinlys clearly asserting herself as a soon-to-be-single woman.

Vanessa's condo surprised him. He'd always assumed she'd buy something as swanky as the penthouses her brothers owned. Vanessa's place was upper-middle class, something a successful law associate might buy, but not what one would expect from an heiress. It didn't even come with a doorman.

A few pots and pans sat in the kitchen along with a set of plates and bowls. It was obvious she'd barely used any of them. The fridge held a few essentials—cream for her coffee and some fruit and yogurt. Justin shook his head. Vanessa needed to eat better.

Her bedroom was simple, with a king-sized bed and pink sheets with small yellow roses and blue hyacinth patterns. Her walk-in closet was full of shoes and clothes without any room for his stuff. He shrugged. She hadn't known he'd be living with her when she'd left the day before.

He showered and changed into a Stanford T-shirt and shorts. It was quite warm in L.A. He'd gone straight to Ceinlys's party after doing some supposedly urgent work. Every time somebody wanted his attention, they threw around the "emergency" label. He made a mental note to shake things up at the office. He wasn't going to babysit his executives, no matter how nervous they were about his replacing Barron. They needed to understand Barron wasn't in charge anymore, and their aim should be to make *him* happy, not his great-uncle.

He sat and reviewed a few items in his inbox. A few minutes later, keys jangled and the door opened and shut. "So you got here okay." Vanessa kicked off her shoes.

"Yup."

She scowled at his phone. "Who are you texting?"

"Just some emails."

Her eyes narrowed. He didn't buy her complaint about how she hadn't liked his shirt, and whatever had been bugging her was still there. "What's wrong?" he asked.

"Nothing."

"Vanessa, it's going to be difficult to be happily married if we aren't honest with each other. I'm trying very hard to be a good husband."

She regarded him. Finally she said, "I don't like blondes."

The pieces fell into place, and he gaped at her. "You're jealous?"

Red flushed her cheeks as her mouth turned flatter than a hyphen. Finally she snapped, "Don't be ridiculous."

"You are!" Absurdly enough he liked her jealous. It meant she felt possessive about him. "You shouldn't have worried."

"Why not?"

"Because no other woman has my wedding band in her jewelry box." He rose and wrapped his arms around her. "You're the first and only."

"Hmph. I hate blondes anyway."

She pulled him down for a hot, carnal kiss. Her mouth attacked his aggressively, and he responded in kind.

Suddenly she broke away. "Take off your clothes."

He pulled the T-shirt over his head and tossed it behind him. His shorts went two seconds later.

"You aren't wearing any underwear." Her pupils darkened as she took him in.

"Saw no reason to."

"Good." She licked her lips.

Justin turned her around and unzipped her dress. The pale violet chiffon pooled at her feet. She was in nothing but a thong, garter belt and a pair of lace-edged stockings that ended at mid-thigh. He cursed as his cock grew so hard it almost hurt. "Is that how you dress on weekends?"

"Depending on what I'm planning." She walked toward him until her bare breasts pressed against his torso. "Right now I want to show you I have more than just your ring." She reached between their bodies and wrapped her hand around his throbbing shaft. He hissed—it felt too damn good, and she hadn't done anything except kiss him and put her hand there.

She rubbed herself against him, her pointed nipples raking his chest. Her cheeks were flushed, and she licked her mouth again.

He crushed her to him and kissed her—almost too roughly, for teasing him and doubting him. Unlike some men, he took his wedding vows seriously. He cupped her ass and squeezed the firm flesh. She gasped, and he stabbed his tongue deep into her mouth, invading her and letting her know who was in charge.

She rocked against him, her hand moving over his cock. His pelvis pumped, and he stopped. "Let go."

"No," she whispered.

"We're not doing this in your living room."

Understanding dawned on her, and she let go. He swung her up, into his arms, and carried her to the bedroom and laid her on the sheet. Her hair spread out, she looked like a wanton angel.

Mine. My wife.

He moved over her and claimed her mouth in a possessive kiss. She wasn't the only one green-eyed with jealousy. She worked in a firm crawling with men—and she wouldn't let anybody know she was already taken. If he hadn't trusted her, he would never have allowed her to keep their marriage a secret.

He ran his finger along the seam of her sex, hot and wet through the thong. He swallowed a groan. It was unbelievable how responsive she was, how sexy.

She gripped his shoulders, her nails digging into his muscles. Her thighs parted, and he fitted himself closer, his mouth fused to hers. He could stay like this forever, pleasuring her and loving her.

Suddenly she pushed him over on his back. She straddled him, her hot core resting over his cock, making it pulse. Her cascading hair looked like a river of fire as she gazed down at him with a feline smile on her lips. "I like you like this. I feel like I can do anything to you."

"So do it," he said, his voice passion-husky.

She raked her nails over his chest, just enough to make him feel the sting. "I believe I will."

VANESSA HAD BEEN STEWING ABOUT HIM AND THE other women at the party, and now that she had him under her, her inner self crowed. She wanted him so turned on that he wouldn't even remember his name.

She traced his body with her mouth. He was so lean and hard all over, his muscles so responsive to her lips. She remembered how much he loved having her hair caress his skin, so she made sure it followed the same path her mouth did.

Her fingernails flicked his nipples—making him gasp—then her tongue laved them one by one to soothe the hurt.

"How does that feel?" she whispered.

"Great."

She hummed gently and pulled a nipple into her mouth, sucking it hard. His breathing roughened, and she smiled with satisfaction. To make sure its twin didn't feel neglected, she rolled it and pinched it with her fingers. His cock grew even harder and it pulsed between her legs. She rocked gently against the hot length, enjoying the slickness her own juices and his pre-cum created between their bodies.

Finally she made her way along his ridged stomach, kissing each section with loving care. Justin always took such good care of his body, and she loved the sheer maleness of it. There was absolutely nothing she would have changed about it.

As she traveled lower, his breathing deepened and became more erratic. Probably he expected her to kiss the blunt head of his penis. Well, that would come, but not just yet.

She cupped his balls, weighing and scratching them gently as she kissed his inner thigh. He groaned. "Vanessa."

"Shhh. Patience."

She moved over to the other side and wrapped her hand around his thick shaft. She could feel blood pulsing through the steel-hard length, and she smiled. Using his pre-cum she ran her thumb along the purple-blue veins along his cock. His hips jerked upward, seeking more of her. She pulled back with a smile. "Not yet."

"Wicked woman."

"No." She shook her head, making sure her hair brushed over his thighs. "What I am is a possessive woman."

Tendons in his neck and joints stood out in stark relief as she moved her hand up and down his shaft, making sure to stimulate the soft flap of skin underneath his head with her thumb. He was close. His body was as tight as a coil under tension.

"Sit on my face," he gasped out.

She stopped. "What?"

"Lose the thong and sit on my face while you do that. I want to taste you when we both come."

Her whole body clenched with need. She stood up and slowly took off her thong, letting the elastic travel down her legs. Justin watched her with dark, glittering eyes. She got back on the bed and straddled him, facing away downstream. This felt a bit more intimate and exposed than him going down on her.

"Move closer," he said, his voice low but no less commanding.

She scooched down until she could feel his breath on her bare ass.

"A little more. I'm so close." His tongue flicked over the lower crease of her butt.

Moaning softly, she slid down toward him, her hips swaying back and forth. His mouth closed over her, and she shut her eyes and arched her back at how good it felt. "God."

"You taste amazing."

"Mmm." She opened her eyes. Justin's cock dripped clear pre-cum all over his tight belly. She ran her hand along his shaft, then she pulled the head of his penis into her mouth.

It was all Justin with a hint of salt. She used her lips and tongue and cheeks and hands to give him pleasure. He braced his feet against the mattress and thrust into her mouth in a controlled way, dipping his head into her mouth then pulling out. Meanwhile his fingers opened her up shamelessly, and he thrummed her clit and stabbed her pussy with his tongue. His cock in her mouth muffled her loud moan, but she was so, sooo close…

He dipped a finger into her, then ran it along the opening of her anus.

"*Justin!*"

She came, clutching his hips to prevent herself from grinding into his face too hard. Her scream echoed against the walls. She felt like even the tip of her hair was tingling from the force of her orgasm.

Justin shifted underneath her, and she found herself flat on her back. He linked his fingers with hers and slowly sank into her. "You have no idea how beautiful you are when you come." He slid easily into her until she felt his balls resting against her bare flesh. "I could watch you come forever."

He kissed her deeply as he moved slowly inside her. Her inner muscles were still shaky from the orgasm, but the feel of him between her legs was like an elixir, and she felt herself starting to build again.

She wrapped her legs around his waist, pulling him closer. He increased his tempo. He had to be close… She'd gotten him so worked up.

He lifted his torso and changed the angle so he could stimulate her clit with every thrust. She gasped as the pleasure began to crescendo again, pushing her closer to the edge once more. He watched her, his eyes passion-glazed. As she gazed up at him, it was like he was a black arts warlock who'd cast a spell on her—to own her completely.

"Come for me, Vanessa."

Her back arched at the darkly whispered command, and she came with a soundless scream. Somehow it was sharper and more intense, like the previous one had just been an appetizer.

Justin groaned as her inner muscles flexed around his cock and he came, his head thrown back. He clenched his teeth, and he looked like a savage god over her.

Rolling so she'd lie on top of him, he wrapped his arms around her. When his breathing slowed, he kissed the back of her neck. "You're a hell of a woman."

She laughed.

"What are you doing tomorrow? If you want, we can fly to Mexico for a one-day honeymoon," he said. "We can take our honeymoon one day a week until we've had our requisite month."

She gasped. "*Month?* Nobody has a honeymoon for a whole month."

He kissed her. "We do. You're worth it."

She gently pushed back the hair that fell over his forehead. "I can't. I have to work tomorrow."

"Boo. It's Sunday."

"I've been taking a lot of days off recently. I have to make up for it somehow. It's a really long shot, but I might be able to make partner this year. I don't want to screw it up."

"Does this mean you'll be billing over a hundred hours a week? I don't think it's healthy for a pregnant woman to work so much."

"I'll be fine. It's not like I'm on my feet all day."

"Still." He put a hand over her belly possessively. "Junior might not like it."

"Junior, is it?" Would he be disappointed if it was a girl?

"We'll see. I don't care, so long as it's healthy."

"You don't want a boy just like Barron?"

Justin shuddered. "One Barron is plenty." Justin brushed the tip of his nose against hers. "I want our child to have the best traits from both of us."

Vanessa smiled. "You're so sweetly sentimental. I never knew."

"Don't tell anybody. It'll ruin my reputation."

Giggling, she snuggled closer…and wished the moment would never end.

ELEVEN

After Vanessa had left for work the next day, Justin pulled out his phone and dialed John Highsmith's personal mobile number.

Justin wasn't a client yet, but Highsmith seemed eager to earn Sterling & Wilson's business. The company needed a new legal team in California, and the firm was one of the best.

"Hello?" Highsmith's voice was smooth but guarded.

"This is Justin Sterling."

"Justin! How good of you to call."

Justin smiled. It was lunchtime on a Sunday. He doubted there was anything good about the timing. "Am I interrupting anything?"

"Not at all."

"Oh, good. There's something I need a little help with."

"If it is within my power," Highsmith said, relishing his vowels. He sounded like he was auditioning for an Elizabethan play.

"I want you to pull Vanessa Pryce off all her cases." *Especially the ones she was working on with Felix Peck.* "I'd like her to work on a special project for us instead."

"That can certainly be arranged."

Justin smiled. Highsmith didn't even try to argue, and he liked that. Lawyers should work to please him. "Have her work no more than forty, but feel free to bill a hundred. Keep my name and the Sterling & Wilson connection out of it—this must be absolutely confidential. You can send a retainer agreement to my office in Chicago. Have it addressed to my assistant."

"It will be my pleasure to do so."

Justin could feel the man crow over the phone. Highsmith was a weasel—a very good one—and he was Justin's weasel now. He would do whatever Justin told him to keep Sterling & Wilson as a client.

Justin hung up, fully satisfied.

VANESSA WENT TO THE OFFICE EARLY. SINCE IT WAS an off day she wore a black T-shirt with a shark across her chest and khaki shorts. A few of the associates working over the weekend were also casually dressed. Felix waved from a conference room, and Vanessa went over.

"Get that shit-eating grin off your face," Felix said. "Highsmith's been looking for you."

Vanessa blinked. "He has?"

"Yeah. It kind of felt urgent."

She cursed under her breath. "You've got to be kidding me." She didn't work closely with him, but she knew his reputation: impatient and exacting. "Why didn't you call?"

"He didn't want me to. He just asked you to join him in his office as soon as you get in."

That's weird. John didn't believe in wasting even a second of his time. Non-billable moments had no place in his life. "Okay. Thanks."

She walked down the hall and stopped in front of the dark wood door with a golden plaque that read: John P. Highsmith. She took a moment to gather her thoughts, then knocked.

"Come in!"

The corner office had a priceless antique mahogany desk with a leather executive chair. The windows had a spectacular view of downtown Los Angeles, and the pristine cream walls had built-in shelves with what probably amounted to a metric ton of leather-bound legal tomes and awards. A sleek silver laptop and a phone took up the right side of his desk, while four accordion folders sat on the left.

"You wanted to see me?"

John nodded, his eyes shrewd. He'd always reminded Vanessa of a big bruiser, the kind of a guy she might see working as a bouncer at a popular club, except he always wore suits no bouncer could afford and a superior smile that said he never lost. Given his reputation, he probably actually *hadn't* lost a lawsuit in at least the last decade.

"Have a seat." He waited until she lowered herself onto a plush armchair across from him. "I understand you're working on the Solaris case?"

"Yes. Harry Dickson assigned me to it, along with Felix."

"Mm. Well, I'm pulling you off it."

She frowned. "Why?"

"It's in the best interests of the firm to do so. You'll be working on a highly confidential case instead."

"Is Harry aware of this?"

"Yes, but he couldn't tell you this in person since he had to fly to Florida. His mother had her monthly crisis."

Harry's mother's "monthly crises" were infamous at the firm. They required her only son to fly to Miami to see her. One time he'd ignored her, and she'd supposedly had a heart attack.

"So who's the client?" Vanessa asked.

"As I said, the case is confidential. So I'm afraid I can't disclose the name."

She raised her eyebrows. "I need to know to do what I do best."

"I understand, but the client's a bit eccentric."

"If I can't even know who the client is, what am I doing?"

"Nothing too complicated. You just need to"—he raised his shoulders in a careless shrug—"review some documents that the in-house counsel's been working on."

"That won't take me any time at all."

"Oh there are quite a lot of them. Fortunately, there's no real rush. So you won't need to work more than forty billable hours a week on this."

"So I can still work on the Solaris case."

"No." John sighed. "The new client will be your only one. For the time being."

"You can't be serious!"

"Vanessa. I assure you, this won't count against you."

"Right." She knew how the game was played. If other people had more billable hours than she did, she'd look bad in July, no matter what John said now. She gave him a hard stare. "Are you doing this because you have somebody else in mind for July?" she asked point-blank.

John started. "What? No, of course not. Don't be ridiculous."

"Then there's no reason for you to take me off the Solaris case. Put somebody else on this new thing. Like Stan."

"Vanessa—"

"You know this is going to hurt me. I've dedicated my life to this firm."

"Yes, I understand that. But I give you my word, this won't be a black mark on your record. Quite the contrary. We'll be counting your billable hours at two and a half times the actual rate. So even though you'll be putting in forty, it will count as a hundred." He spread his hands and beamed at her.

Vanessa gasped. "You can't do that. That's unethical."

John's smile collapsed. "I'm aware of the ethical aspects, thank you. This is what the client wants."

"The client told you to limit the work to forty hours, but to bill them for a hundred?"

"Correct."

"And you expect me to believe this?"

He leaned forward, his previous bonhomie gone. "I don't care what you believe. I expect you to follow my instructions. And before you think about reporting me to the bar, everything I've said in this room is true. If you cause trouble, you'll end up jobless. Most likely you'll have to start fresh at some other firm…assuming you can find one that will have you." He waved her away. "Now run along. Everything you need to look at is in Conference Room 2B."

Fists clenched, she left. *What a bunch of…* John had to be lying through his teeth.

Or did he? She thought about it, her feet slowing as she walked down the hall. The firm was doing great. He was doing great. There was no reason to risk tarnishing the firm's reputation, much less his own. And Vanessa had never seen him lie to an associate before. Why would he start now?

On her way to the conference room, she stopped by Felix's desk. "I can't believe it."

He gave her a concerned look. "What happened?"

"He put me on another case."

"Seriously?"

"Yeah. And he won't say who the client is or anything."

"That's weird."

"Right? Anyway, so I'm doing—" she shrugged helplessly " —something. I have no idea what. Have you heard…?"

"Nope. Not a thing. I had no idea he was going to pull you off the case. Otherwise I would've waited until you finished the deposition," he joked lamely.

She made a face. "I'll send you everything I have."

"Thanks." Felix hesitated. "Look, I just want you to know that the work you're going to do is important, even though it might look sort of lame at the moment."

She tilted her head. "You know something I don't? Or are you just trying to make me feel better?"

"Hey, just saying. Nothing this firm does is inconsequential. You know that better than anyone." He flashed a quick smile.

She nodded with a smile of her own. "Yeah, and we all know there's no news in the firm you don't hear first."

He waved it away, but it was true. He was popular among the secretaries, and they loved to include him in their gossip. Maybe somebody had let it slip that the work really *was* important.

Conference room 2B had a big desk and two plastic chairs. It wasn't one of the fancier ones since it was a work room, not a "shock and awe the clients" room.

She opened a leather folio. Inside was a computer print out that read: *Review and file in chronological order*. She stared at the ten boxes in front of her. This had to be some sick joke. This was the kind of work you might give to an intern, not an associate. Had she pissed off one of the partners or their cronies?

The documents' letterheads were blacked out. She glared at the papers and started reading them. Just because the partners were determined to screw her didn't mean she had to roll over. She wasn't giving them any reason to ruin her eval come July.

The back of her neck prickled like a centipede was crawling across it. She turned and saw John tapping his Rolex at her. "You've got to be kidding me," she muttered as he jerked his chin toward the door.

If he wanted her gone, fine. She'd leave. She picked up her phone and texted Justin. *Have you had lunch yet?*

Not yet.

Let's have Chinese then. Order me sweet and sour pork and fried rice. I'm heading home now.

JUSTIN GLANCED AT VANESSA'S TEXT AND RAN HIS teeth across his lip. Hmm. That didn't sound good. He padded barefoot to her kitchen, looking for a menu. She must have one from her favorite Chinese delivery.

He didn't have to wait long after placing their order. Vanessa showed up, her eyes flashing fury and her mouth flat and disapproving. If their lives were drawn in a cartoon, steam would've been hissing out of her ears.

"I thought you were going to be at the office all day," he said conversationally. If Highsmith had screwed up, Justin was going to kill him.

"Well, things have changed." She tossed her purse and briefcase on the couch and started pacing. Her jaw muscles worked as she clenched her teeth. "That jerk pulled me off the case."

"What case?"

"An important one. That's all I can say."

"Maybe they had an even more important task for you to do."

"No. They put me on something that should be an intern's job. Seriously. Filing stuff in chronological order? And this mythical client wants to pay more than twice my billing rate? I don't think so."

Justin scratched the tip of his nose. "What's so unbelievable about that?"

"Because it's stupid to pay that much! Besides, I can't waste my life filing when I should be working on important cases and make sure the partners know how valuable I am to the firm. I need to show what a great lawyer I am, how I can charm clients and win more business. You know, things like that."

"If you want to bring in business, why don't you use your family connections?"

"*Because I'm not going to climb the ladder of family connections to the top like some brainless moneyed idiot!*" she burst out, then clicked her mouth shut. Flushing, she blinked a few times. "Maybe it makes me sound arrogant," she began, her words slow and measured, "but I want to do it on my own. I want my career to be…entirely mine. Dane, you rat bastard." Suddenly she buried her flushed face in her hands.

Justin didn't know how her oldest brother figured into all this, but he could guess. As if being an asshole wasn't enough, Dane was very good at manipulating people, somewhat like Barron. Justin pulled Vanessa down onto the couch and held her.

"Every family has a rat bastard," he said, tucking tendrils of her hair behind her ears.

She laughed humorlessly. "But not like Dane. He played me all along, egging me on, telling me I could never be a partner on my own. And I wanted to prove him wrong so bad I spent the last ten years of my life doing exactly that."

"Isn't partnership what you want though?"

"Yes," she answered reflexively, then shook her head. "Maybe." She huffed. After a moment, she added quietly, "I don't know. I just wanted to do it on my own."

That Justin could understand. Her family was wealthy and influential, and he bet it cast a long shadow everywhere she went. He didn't see anything wrong with her wanting to be free of that. He'd always had the same desire himself.

He felt slightly bad about his role in her getting put on the "boring" work, but he couldn't believe Highsmith hadn't done a better job of spinning the work so it sounded ridiculously important. Like it was an *honor* to be on it.

Maybe he should have a quick conversation with the partner. Highsmith was to make sure Vanessa didn't work too much, not piss her off by giving her scut work.

Their lunch arrived; Justin paid and brought it to the dining table. He'd ordered egg drop soup as well since she liked it, and settled down to decimate his Kung Pao chicken.

Vanessa chewed her pork. She seemed to have a good appetite now. Maybe the morning sickness the day before had been an aberration. Women threw up during pregnancy, but it couldn't be optimal to lose one's food when eating for two.

"Are you doing any work today?" she asked.

"No." He'd cleared his calendar until Monday.

"What were you planning to do all day?"

"Oh, this and that." He gave her a wicked smile. "Why?"

"Now that I can't work, I don't know what to do with myself."

He chuckled. "I can think of a few things." He washed down his chicken with Coke. "Actually, I was going to take a nice hot shower…while thinking about you."

She raised an eyebrow like she wasn't affected, but her eyes where darker now. "Is thinking all you were going to do?"

He winked. "I don't fist and tell. But I'll let you watch."

She licked her lips. "Seriously?"

"Seriously."

"Now?"

"Now."

TWELVE

VANESSA COULDN'T BELIEVE HOW TURNED on she was at the idea that he masturbated while fantasizing about her. She was slick and tingly between her legs, like they hadn't done the dirty-and-sweaty the night before.

Justin started the water in the shower. Her master bathroom had a separate shower stall encased in glass. He brought a stool in. "Sit."

She plopped down. He stripped off his shirt. Her breath caught at the hard, rippling muscles on his back and torso. The bright light showcased all his masculine perfection. He got rid of his shorts and underwear, and she pulled her lips in at how hard he was already. Long and thick, his shaft stood up, the head of his cock so close to his flat stomach.

He strutted around, shamelessly flaunting his body. He was gorgeous, his movements gracefully economical, like an athlete in his prime.

With a grin, he went inside the stall. The water sluiced down his body in rivulets, tracing every line. He shampooed his thick dark hair, and white suds skimmed down his strong back. He grabbed a bar of soap and ran it over his body.

"I think of you all the time, constantly." His voice was low but clear over the sound of running water. "You come to me at the most inopportune moments at times, but it always makes me happy to think of you."

One big, strong hand wrapped around his shaft, and Vanessa forgot to breathe. She'd never considered herself very visual or a Peeping Jane, but watching Justin start to pleasure himself with his eyes on her made her go instantly wet.

The water droplets beaded on the glass, and the steam fogged it, making it harder to see him, but it didn't matter. It only added to the surreal sexiness.

"Take off your shirt," he said, as his fist moved slowly up and down. "Let me see you."

Keeping her eyes on him, she took it off. At his rough intake of breath, she grew bolder and undid the front clasp of her bra and let it slide down her arms and fall.

"Jesus."

"I want to see you come, Justin," Vanessa said, her mouth dry. She couldn't believe how brazen she was—completely out of character. But it was so freeing to watch him hard like this for her.

His ass tightened as he pumped into his fist, his eyes on her. "Play with your tits," he said, his voice rough. "Imagine it's my hands on you. *Now*."

She cupped her bare breasts. They were fuller than before and more sensitive. She grazed the pointed nubs with her thumbs and gasped as an electric sensation shot through her, leaving her tingling all over. She pressed her legs together, feeling the aching emptiness there.

"Fondle them the way I would," he said, his thrusts faster now.

Swallowing hard, she remembered the way he liked to play with her breasts, shaping them, testing their softness and teasing their tips until she moaned and writhed underneath him. It felt ten times naughtier to do it to herself while Justin watched. Her hands were softer and smaller than Justin's, but the effect was the same. Maybe it was the intensity of his gaze as it followed her hands; she felt branded to the core.

"Slip your hand inside your panties and play with yourself. Put your fingers inside yourself and pretend it's my cock fucking you."

Beyond caring now, she did as he asked. Her clit was so wet and swollen, and she was so primed it was easy to slip two fingers in. He cursed and whispered dark encouragements. "Yes, baby, that's it. Make yourself feel so fucking good."

She watched him through slitted eyes. He was close, she could tell. But he was holding back, his formidable control not letting him go. The plump head peeked out every time his fist pumped, and she licked her lips at how it glistened.

"God, I wish I was doing this with your cock in my mouth," she said.

Justin's face twisted as his control shattered. He shouted as he ejaculated in a long, ropey spurt. She watched it, absolutely mesmerized at the way pleasure tightened his face. His hand on the wall fisted, and he rested his head against the foggy glass, his eyes on her.

A moment later, he straightened and turned off the water. The glass door opened, and he came out, water beaded on his skin. "You haven't come yet."

"No." Her hand was still between her legs, but she hadn't done anything to push herself over the edge. She'd been too enthralled by his performance.

He pulled her up, getting water on her bare torso. She moaned as his chest rubbed against her nipples. It was incredible to have him on her like this. He unbuckled her shorts and dragged them and her underwear off in one impatient movement. He took her wrist and brought her wet hand to his mouth and sucked the juices off her fingers. "You taste amazing."

With a jerk, he perched her at the edge of the double vanity. The marble was cold against her heated skin. He dropped to his knees before her and inhaled her scent. "I can never get enough of you."

He pushed her thighs wide and breathed gently over the slick, pink flesh. "You're too damn hot." He buried his face between her legs and feasted on her, his mouth ravenous. Pleasure spread through her, and her toes curled. She threw her head back, her fingers buried in his wet hair. The man was irresistible, his lips and tongue and teeth always knowing exactly what she needed the most.

Ecstasy coiled inside her, and she clenched her teeth to contain a groan. A sheen of sweat covered her, and she became desperate, so close to what she wanted.

He sucked on her clit hard, pushing three fingers inside her. The invasion was nothing like her smaller and more delicate digits.

"I'm coming," she moaned.

His response was to pump his fingers faster and suck even harder on her clit. She screamed his name as an orgasm seared its way through her. Her nerve endings felt fried; she couldn't have remembered her name as Justin licked and kissed her on the way back down.

"Oh wow…" She fell forward and her hands gripped his shoulders as the bathroom spun. She blinked a few times. What was that about?

"Are you okay?" he peered at her.

"I'm fine. Just a great orgasm." She laughed, unwilling to ruin the moment. The momentary dizziness was probably nothing. "So what else are you planning to do now that you've showered?"

His grin was pure wickedness. "Why don't I show you?"

JUSTIN ROLLED HIS SHOULDERS AFTER REPLYING TO his marketing department's latest proposal with a large red exclamation mark. Maybe it would've been easier to hire monkeys to do their job because that was about the level of deliverables coming from them. They were scared of screwing up—he got that. But he hadn't hired them to copy what everyone else was doing.

Hopefully his response would generate the results he wanted. If not, he had no problem replacing the entire department. He'd done it once already, with another department, and he could do it again. Nobody was irreplaceable.

He plowed through the rest of the initiatives and proposals. He couldn't wait to wrap up everything so he could fly to L.A. The previous seven weeks had been some of the best of his life. Who would've thought marriage would agree with him so perfectly?

"Sir, your brother's here," came Rita's voice over the intercom.

"Send him in."

Nate was a couple of years younger than Justin, but he'd never shown any interest in running Sterling & Wilson. If there had been even a hint of such interest, Barron would've plucked him out of his happy life and molded him into what he considered to be "executive material."

Nate appeared in an expensive shirt and slacks. He dressed with more care when he visited Sterling & Wilson, apparently to maintain the image Barron wanted of him. Justin leaned back in his seat. "What's up?"

"What I was gonna ask you." Nate took a seat. "What *are* you up to these days?"

"Busy. You know."

"Hmm. Yeah. With the sudden relocation to San Francisco and all. You hate the city."

"I get tired of the weather in Chicago."

Nate snorted. "Yeah, right. If you liked it any colder and nastier you'd be a penguin."

"Okay. Which one of them have been whining to you?"

"All of them." Nate sighed. "I don't know why they think I can influence you in any way. They're better off begging Barron."

Justin scowled. The executives trying to figure out whether they should please Barron or him were annoying as hell. Barron was in Maryland full-time now. That meant it was Justin who was in charge.

It might have been easier if Barron had made his retirement official, but that old dog hadn't done that yet. If he'd been a petty man, Justin might have thought his great-uncle was delaying on purpose. But most likely Barron just didn't think it mattered—that it was the executives' job to figure out who was in charge and behave accordingly.

"But I'm not really worried about the executives," Nate said. "I'm wondering why you're flying to L.A. every night."

"Are you stalking me?"

"Ha. No, I read the auditors' report and talked to your pilot. You know we have a corporate penthouse in the city, right?"

Justin scowled. He hadn't expected his pilot to talk, but then again he hadn't bothered to swear the man to secrecy. A mistake he wouldn't make again. "Got things to do in L.A."

Nate chortled. "Things, or a girl? She must be super hot to have you flying out every night. I don't remember you acting this bad, not even with Vanessa." He knew about Justin's on-and-off relationship with her. "And V's hot with a capital H."

Justin tried for a bland expression. Telling his brother to watch his mouth wouldn't do any good, and he'd promised to keep the marriage quiet until July. "You know, I actually do have work to do. Why don't you go visit Kerri? See how she is? She's pregnant, you know."

"Oh yeah, I know. Don't worry, she's doing fine. She has Ethan, the prototypical over-protective husband, plus her sister- and mother-in-law fawning over her. Barron, too."

"I almost feel sorry for her," Justin said. "Barron must be impossible to deal with."

"I think Ethan's doing a pretty good job of handling him." Nate tapped his lip. "It's going to be you next, you know."

"Me?"

"Baby."

Justin narrowed his eyes, wondering if Nate suspected something.

"You're the Heir Apparent, so it's your duty, hahaha. Barron's already muttering about it. Carry on the family legacy, and all that. I'm not interested, of course. Gonna be single forever and leech off my inheritance." Nate smiled like a cat with a bowl of fresh cream. "Anyway, I'm leaving now. Got a party to catch."

Which explained why he was in San Francisco.

"And if you want to keep your little affair a secret," Nate leaned in from the doorway and affected a stage whisper, "you might not want to expense the trips." He left, waving a hand.

Justin cursed. Rita generally took care of his expenses—personal and otherwise—and she'd probably assumed his trips to L.A. were work-related. Besides, her default mode when it came to his expenses was to assign them to Sterling & Wilson. He made a mental note to talk to her about that. Hopefully Barron was too distracted to read the auditors' report carefully. He didn't want his great-uncle wondering what he was up to.

"So tell me how you have the time to join us for yoga," Hilary asked, doing a final stretch on her mat. Sweat from the session glistened on her skin.

Jane nodded. "Yeah. I thought you were the career-minded one."

"Oh, I am." Vanessa sat up. "But now I'm on strict orders not to work more than forty hours a week. And everyone at the firm hates me." Well, not quite everyone, but it was pretty close. And the feeling wasn't always hate. Many of them pitied her, convinced she was going to get screwed in July. She shared the sentiment, despite what John had said.

"Why can't you work overtime?" Hilary asked.

"No idea." But the work had gotten a bit more challenging. Now she was writing a series of articles on some of the finer points of sexual harassment.

"That's weird," Jane said. "But Iain told me you work too much, so maybe your firm is trying to help you not burn out."

"Hah. It is to laugh. Believe me, Highsmith, Dickson and Associates doesn't care about burned-out associates." Any associate who burned out was welcome to leave. If they didn't leave on their own, the firm "counseled them out"—a nicer term to describe a pink slip.

"Is this a subtle hint to get you to do more pro bono?" Hilary asked.

Vanessa snorted. "Doubtful. The partners think I do too much volunteer stuff as it is, except they don't say that out loud because they don't want to sound like jerks. The second I pick up a juicy pro bono case is one half-second before they dump an important 'one hundred and twenty hours a week' case on me." She sighed softly. "It doesn't matter. At least I got a good workout with you guys."

"Definitely." Hilary nodded. "And hey, I think it's great that you're working fewer hours. You positively *glow* these days."

Vanessa forced a smile. If they only knew! "Hilary...do you mind if I ask you a personal question?"

"Go ahead."

Vanessa hesitated. It seemed a little rude to bring up the past, when Hilary had run the other way from Mark, but this was important. Now that she had so much free time, all she did was google Justin's old girlfriends and dates and mull over those gorgeous women, thereby proving the saying about idle hands true. But she couldn't help herself.

She knew, intellectually, that she was pretty, thanks to her mother. But all the others who buzzed around Justin had won a similar genetic jackpot. How could he resist all those beauties? Her father hadn't been able to, not when he was married to one of the most gorgeous women of her generation, not when he'd professed to love her.

Swallowing, Vanessa chose her words carefully. "Mark's reputation's always been pretty bad when it came to relationships..."

Hilary laughed. "That's putting it mildly."

"So... what made you sure he'll be different with you?"

"He loves me."

"That's it?"

Hilary shrugged. "That's all I need to know." She leaned closer. "Why? Are you having issues?"

"No, not at all." Vanessa wasn't telling Hilary and Jane about her secret marriage. "Just wondering if you had some kind of concrete proof. I mean, how can we know for certain what's in people's hearts?"

"Sometimes it's just a matter of trust. If I didn't believe him, I wouldn't be with him, no matter how many times he told me he loved me."

Vanessa scraped her bottom lip with her teeth. Hilary spoke so beautifully and bravely. But unlike her, Vanessa didn't have the courage to make that leap of faith. The sweeter and more magnetic Justin acted, the greater her fear grew—the day might come when she wouldn't be able to derive a drop of happiness without him. Would she become one of those women she saw in her pro-bono work—the ones who put their men's approval and happiness over everything else, including their own children's welfare? Cold terror brushed her as the possibility unfolded in her mind. To be so…*dependent*… "I'm going to get some water and go home. How about you?"

"I'm heading out too. I have a lot of work to do tomorrow," Hilary said.

"Ditto," Jane said.

Hilary worked for one of the richest and busiest men in the world, and Jane was becoming better known as a private chef. Vanessa stopped herself from asking how Hilary could have faith in Mark, knowing his history as an impossible playboy. Even though Hilary was the perfect person to talk to about her doubts, Vanessa didn't know how to broach the subject while keeping her own marriage secret.

She waved them good-bye and went to the water fountain. She peed more now, but was also thirstier than usual. Her doctor had advised her to make sure she wasn't dehydrated.

Vanessa waited for her turn. A willowy brunette in front of her started to put water into a bottle. She turned around. Freckles dotted her face, and her nose was just a tad too large for the rest of her features. "Hi. Sorry, my bottle's sort of big."

Vanessa smiled. "No problem. You were in the yoga class, right?"

"Yeah. I figured I'd join to meet some people. I'm new in town." The brunette's plump pink lips curved into a shy smile. "I'm Peggy Teeter."

"Vanessa. Where are you from?"

"Provo. In Utah? I got a job in L.A., so I moved out here about three weeks ago. It's so different here, and it's not always easy to make friends." She flushed. "Oh my gosh, look at me babbling. Sorry."

"Not a problem. I know how it can be when you're new."

Peggy moved aside when the bottle was full.

Vanessa started filling hers. "My brother just got engaged. Next time, I'll introduce you to his fiancée. She's not from around here either, and I'm sure she'd appreciate a friend."

Watching Vanessa leave the studio, Peggy drew in a long, steadying breath. She'd thought Vanessa would be spoiled and snotty given how she'd grown up and what Stan had said, but she was actually really nice. Peggy had wanted to ask to talk with her privately, but for some reason hadn't been able to. Nice or not, something about Vanessa intimidated her.

Peggy recalled Vanessa's look of pure concentration when they'd been doing the yoga. She was all class and money and unbelievably beautiful. Even without any makeup post-shower, she was still stunning. If she hadn't become a lawyer, she could've been in fashion magazines. Nobody would believe she and Peggy had anything in common.

But there was something. Even if Vanessa had everything Peggy didn't.

She swallowed bitterness. Ceinlys thought she could be stingy and get away with it. She'd soon learn otherwise.

JUSTIN WAS HOME BY THE TIME VANESSA RETURNED from the yoga studio. He was in a dress shirt and slacks, his tie loose. She smiled to herself at how sexy and handsome he looked, then she pulled back and tried to study him with a more objective eye. No matter how hard she searched, there was no hint of meanness, just solid security and something that was too big and deep to be called mere affection. He would love his child to pieces and… And just maybe he'd love her one day too.

"You seem to be in a pretty good mood," he said.

"I got to exercise with Hilary and Jane."

"Nothing too strenuous?"

"Yoga. Not that bad." She kissed him on the mouth. "Have you eaten?"

"No."

"Let's get some Chinese then."

"Again?"

"What can I say? I'm craving sweet and sour pork with fried rice."

Justin raised a hand in surrender, pulled out his phone and ordered Chinese for two.

She cleared her throat. "I have something to show you." She dug through her purse and found the print-out of the baby. "Here. From the visit from this afternoon." She handed it over and shifted, leaning close.

As he looked at the tiny dot, awed happiness suffused his expression. Her heart squeezed, and she almost couldn't breathe.

"I can't believe how small he is," he whispered, his voice full of reverence. "And…he's such a handsome dot."

He reached for her and held her tightly. She hugged him back, her eyes closed as she savored the sweetness of the moment.

"Dr. Silverman said everything's progressing well," she murmured.

"How good is this doctor?"

"Very. She delivered Gavin and Amanda's baby."

Justin nodded. Gavin Lloyd was a billionaire who insisted on nothing but the absolute best for his wife. "I wish I had been able to go with you."

Vanessa squeezed his hand. Her phone beeped, but she ignored it. Probably just work. She sighed, wondering if she was being overly insistent about her promotion being all on her own merit. At the same time she couldn't help but mull over the fact that John put her on a series of odd assignments. Perhaps he was testing her to see if she'd use her connections to make him stop or something.

If she'd brought in her family's or the Sterlings' business, maybe he would quit driving her insane. On the other hand, she didn't want to get promoted based on that. She never wanted anybody to wonder if she had become successful because of her family. She'd worked too damn hard to allow that kind of talk.

"Who spat in your soup?" Justin asked.

"What?"

"You looked like somebody spat in your soup."

"It's nothing."

She didn't want to talk about it with Justin in case he decided to "help" by intervening with her partners. He'd become extremely protective recently. The one good thing about only working forty hours was that it preempted Justin from calling the firm and telling the partners that they were driving her too hard. A sudden thought crossed her mind, but she dismissed it immediately. Not even Justin would be able to make Highsmith put a perfectly good associate on a forty-hour week schedule. If the mystery client wanted to pay a hundred hours for only forty of real work, Highsmith would have had her put in the remaining sixty on other cases. There was always something to do at the firm.

"Really. I'm fine," she added when Justin looked skeptical.

"Okay. Hey, have you thought about moving?"

"No… Why?"

"The place is too small for a family of three. And I know we haven't talked about it, but I think you should get someone to come in for housekeeping. Maybe once a week or so."

She made a face. "You're risking the couch, you know, with your thinly-veiled criticism."

He laughed. "Just thought it'd make your life easier. It's going to get harder and harder for you to move around."

"Let me think about moving. But in the meantime, I guess we can have housekeeping." Actually Vanessa had been wanting to scrub the place from top to bottom. She just never had much time after work and yoga, and she didn't want to waste her evenings with Justin.

"That wasn't so hard, was it? We'll find a trustworthy service that can come in, clean and do the laundry and so on while you're at work."

"Perfect. You think of everything."

"Somebody's got to." He kissed her. "You have no idea how anxious it makes me that we can't announce to everyone we're married already. If I had it my way, you'd be on leave from the firm to rest with your feet up all day long."

"You're sweet when you get all protective. But the doctor said it's okay for me to work. Apparently it's actually good that I get out and not bore myself to death. The baby can feel my moods. I don't want a bad one to affect it."

"That doesn't mean I'm going to quit worrying. You don't know what you and this baby mean to me."

When he spoke like that, she could almost forget her doubts about their future and impending motherhood. She snuggled close to him and held his hand. Was this what a good, loving relationship was supposed to feel like? She tightened her grip on him. "I'll be careful, Justin."

THIRTEEN

VANESSA WENT TO THE OFFICE THE NEXT morning. Justin had left early, promising to come back as soon as he could. Now that she couldn't work weekends, he'd reintroduced the idea of flying to Mexico for a getaway. She'd agreed. She was going stir-crazy without anything to do at the firm.

"Hi, Zoe," Vanessa said to her secretary, but Zoe didn't even raise her head to say hi back. She was staring at her monitor in rapt absorption. "Zoe?"

"Oh my gosh! I didn't see you." Zoe put a hand on her chest. "Did you hear the news?"

"What news?"

"There's been an accident. A private jet lost control and skidded off the runway in San Francisco and crashed into a crane."

"A crane? At the airport?"

"It says they were doing some expansion work."

A cold dread formed in her belly. "Whose plane?"

"Justin Sterling's."

Spots swam in front of her. Her knees buckled, but she caught herself against a filing cabinet. They'd just kissed each other good bye only a few hours ago. She couldn't believe it might have been their last one.

Zoe jumped to her feet and grabbed Vanessa. "Are you all right? Vanessa?"

She blinked, trying to clear her vision. "Did anyone…were there any survivors?"

"So far only one seriously injured, and two with minor injuries. They didn't say anything else."

"Nobody…died?"

"I guess not. I don't know." Zoe's face was filling her vision, looking concerned. "Here." She handed Vanessa a tissue. "Wipe your tears."

"Oh." Vanessa hadn't realized she'd been crying.

"Do you know Justin?"

Vanessa nodded.

Zoe's face tightened. "I hope he's all right."

"Thanks."

Vanessa managed to drag herself to her office, locking her door. She was shaking so violently that she finally collapsed on the carpeted floor, feeling like she was going to throw up. Was it Justin who was seriously injured?

Hands over her belly, she rolled onto her side. This was all her fault. She'd been so resentful of his high-handed act in Chicago that she'd insisted on keep their marriage secret, claiming she didn't want her in-laws to affect her career. Now that she thought about it, she could've just told her partners she wouldn't be used to bring in her in-laws' business either. If her refusal to persuade her family to bring its business to the firm hadn't hurt her, a refusal to get the Sterlings for Highsmith, Dickson and Associates wouldn't have either.

Her fault, her fault.

She pressed a fist against her mouth, trying to muffle a sob.

My god…Justin…

She should google for updates on the accident. But every time she tried to sit up, nausea hit her. She lay back on the floor and prayed harder than she'd ever prayed before.

Justin paced in the hospital. His pilot was seriously injured, while he and the cabin attendant had some bruises. There would be an investigation into what had actually caused the accident, but he was certain it was due to the poor visibility at the airport with thick and heavy fog.

He wanted to call Vanessa, but he'd forgotten to charge his phone the night before, and there was no juice. And now they were keeping him at this damn hospital.

"I'm fine," he told the doctor again.

"We have to make sure," the man said. A pair of rimless glasses sat on his long, pale face. "You may feel okay at the moment, but you might have other injuries you may not be aware of."

"People are going to worry."

"We notified your brother, Mr. Sterling. And I'm sure your family will be just as relieved to hear you were a model patient."

The doctor was smiling, but Justin wasn't in the mood for levity. Nate didn't know about Vanessa, and she would undoubtedly hear about the accident. Hopefully she wouldn't worry too much. "Fine. Make it quick."

The doctor scheduled an MRI and CAT scan among other things. Justin wanted to bang his head against the wall, but he couldn't blame the man for being thorough. He knew who Justin was. If anything happened to Justin because of medical negligence, Barron Sterling would descend upon the hospital with a horde of lawyers. Everyone knew what a vindictive asshole Barron could be.

It wasn't until noon that the doc finally told him what he already knew. "It's a miracle." Still the doctor prescribed some painkillers, just in case Justin felt sore, and discharged him.

"To your office, sir?" his chauffeur asked.

"No. To the airport."

His chauffeur drove extra slowly, testing Justin's patience. He reined in his temper, and called his assistant from the car phone. "Rita—"

"Oh my gosh, Justin, are you all right?"

"I'm fine, but my laptop's toast. Ship a replacement to my address in L.A. Make sure it gets there before COB today. And I need a new charger. Have it waiting for me at SFO." He didn't have Vanessa's number memorized—an oversight that was going to be corrected ASAP—and his personal cell was the only phone that had it.

"Anything else?"

"Cancel all my appointments for today and tomorrow. If anybody calls, I'm not in. And get me on the first flight to L.A."

VANESSA ENDED UP GOING HOME, WHERE SHE SAT trembling in front of the TV. None of the news stations had anything about the crash in San Francisco. She googled, but that didn't yield much either. Everything was speculative—one early report said a man had died, then published a correction. It seemed like nobody knew what was really going on. *Probably more interested in posting something first*, she thought angrily, *rather than something accurate.*

Frustrated, she undid her hair and started pacing. Jittery energy and tension gripped her. Even now Justin's family might be preparing for a funeral.

She hugged herself. No. She wouldn't be negative.

But she still hadn't heard anything about the accident, and his phone kept forwarding her to the voice mail. Surely, if Justin was okay, he would've called.

Maybe there was some other reason why he couldn't call. Maybe he'd lost his phone in the accident. She picked up her phone and scrolled through her contacts. The names of clients, friends and colleagues flashed by. Her family probably didn't know any better than her, and she didn't know the numbers for Justin's family.

Of course, she could find it easily enough. But it seemed awkward to call one of the Sterling & Wilson offices and ask, "Hey, did Justin survive?"

She was Justin's wife. She should be the first one to know. And if she hadn't been so damn insistent about keeping their relationship secret, she would have been.

Keys jangled at the door, and she turned sharply. Justin walked in, and for a moment her brain couldn't process what it was seeing.

"Hey," Justin said, opening his arms.

"You're not dead!" She jumped into his arms, linking her hands behind his neck. "You're not dead."

"I'm fine, baby. I'm fine." He wiped his thumbs over her cheeks, and she realized once again that she'd been crying.

"I thought… I couldn't reach you and nobody knew anything."

"I know, I'm so sorry. I forgot to charge my phone last night."

She shook her head. "No, it's all okay now. Are you hurt?"

"Nah. A couple of bruises, nothing to talk about. It's almost a miracle."

She pressed her palms against his cheeks and brought his head down for a kiss. She couldn't believe he was with her, healthy and whole.

Thank you, thank you, thank you.

He kissed her back, his mouth desperate for her, and she poured her soul into the moment.

Without breaking the kiss, he carried her to the bedroom. They stripped each other out of their clothes, hands hurried and clumsy. His fingers tunneled into her hair, coiling it around them. He gripped her pelvis, and she spread her legs, wanting to feel him inside her so much, to know he was really here with her.

He pushed into her, his thick cock gliding into her right where it belonged. There was no slow savoring, just desperate relief and joy that they had cheated death.

He adjusted the angle, grinding into her sensitive nub with every thrust. Legs wrapped around him, she held onto his wide, solid shoulders, and sobbed out her relief and pleasure.

He let go, his face stark in climax. She put her hand against his flushed cheek.

Mine.

AFTER A FEW MOMENTS JUSTIN ROLLED OFF SO HE wouldn't crush her. She turned to face him, her hair spread around her. "Justin…"

"Yeah?"

"I don't think it's working."

Something cold wedged in his heart, turning the post-orgasm glow to ashes. "What do you mean?" he asked, keeping his voice neutral.

"It drove me crazy, not knowing. When nobody contacted me. If people knew I was your wife, they would've called me first."

"That's true."

"So…maybe we should out ourselves. You know, announce the marriage. Then we could've avoided all this. You wouldn't have to sneak around or risk your life."

Justin smoothed a hand over her creased forehead. "This wasn't your fault. It was the weather. The Bay area can get pretty foggy. Visibility was poor, and my pilot made a mistake. It's not like I'm flying into a battle zone every day."

"Still—"

"I'm serious. I know how important this July is for you. Didn't you say you wanted to get promoted based on your own merits, and not because you're married to me?"

"Yeah, but it doesn't matter. I'm not getting promoted this year."

He pulled back slightly. "You're not?"

She shook her head. "The partners are giving me BS work. They also aren't letting me do more than forty hours a week. You know what that means at a law firm?" She didn't wait for his response. "It's a not-so-subtle hint that I have no future there."

Put it that way, it did look pretty bad. But he'd done it to ensure she wouldn't work too much, and he didn't want to change the way things were, not even to appease her self-esteem. A hundred billable hours a week was ridiculous for a pregnant woman. When would she find the time to see her doctor or eat regularly? He remembered how Gavin Lloyd's wife had a pregnancy scare, and the woman had *staff* waiting on her. "Have they said anything to you directly?"

"No, but…"

"Well, you know what happens when you assume. Maybe your partners have a reason."

"I guess." She sighed, as though in resignation, but her thoughts were going a mile a minute from the way her eyes flashed.

"Hey. It's okay. Everything's going to be fine."

She smiled. "You're right. What do I have to complain about when you're back safe and sound?"

He smiled back, swallowing the guilt twisting his gut.

FOURTEEN

THE NEXT MORNING, VANESSA THOUGHT that maybe she'd spoken too soon.

Zoe greeted her with, "Harry and John are looking for you. They want to see you immediately. In the Grand Conference Room."

Vanessa raised an eyebrow. It was the nicest one the firm had, the one the partners used to impress new recruits and clients. She walked briskly down the hall, getting a few strange looks along the way. They barely registered. Strange looks were becoming almost normal, now that she was working so little.

She stopped in front of the dark wood door and took a deep breath. *The Grand Conference Room isn't designed for layoffs. You'll be okay.*

She knocked once and went inside. The conference room had a long mahogany table with expensive leather chairs. The windows gave a panoramic view of downtown Los Angeles, and the pristine cream walls had built-in shelves that held strategically placed awards and photos of the partners posing with various VIPs. It had been designed to impress.

Neither Harry nor John sat at the head of the table. Oh no. That seat currently belonged to another, far more important person: Barron Sterling.

Vanessa paused. Despite his age, Barron looked as languid and deadly as a great white shark. Fortunately his eyes twinkled with something that looked like good humor. She wondered about it for a split-second before remembering that it had to be because Justin had survived the crash. *Totally understandable.*

A Saville Row suit encased his solid body, only a hint of softness around the middle betraying his advanced years. He toyed with a sugar cookie that was on a plate in front of him.

Vanessa nodded to him and turned to the partners. "You were looking for me?"

"Yes." John glanced at his watch. "For the last twenty-six minutes."

She flushed. "I wish you'd called."

"Nonsense," Barron said, his gaze turning flinty as he glanced at John. "I'd never let anybody disturb my niece's morning."

She blinked a few times. "Your niece?"

Barron wiped his hands clean and rose. Facing her, he spread his arms. "Welcome to the family, Vanessa."

She stared at Barron, then at the partners. The latter looked quite pleased. They were actually beaming at her like she was a prize race-horse who'd just won the triple crown.

"Mr. Sterling, I think there's been a mistake," Vanessa said thinly. Despite her suggestion to make their marriage public the night before, she was certain Justin hadn't gone ahead and told his great-uncle. He knew how Barron was.

"Nonsense. I don't make mistakes. And please, call me Barron."

No mistakes? She bit the inside of her cheek. She could think of a few times, but mentioning them now wouldn't be prudent.

Barron continued, "My only objection to all this is that you didn't invite me to the wedding. Despite what you might've heard, I make a marvelous wedding guest."

"I'm sure," she said automatically. Her stomach suddenly started churning. "Excuse me," she said, then bolted from the conference room.

John yelled from behind her, and Barron muttered something. She couldn't make out anything, her ears ringing. She reached the bathroom and emptied her stomach.

She rinsed and wiped her mouth. Her cheeks looked flushed, matching the apple red of her hair, but otherwise she was deathly pale. She put a hand to her forehead. How could Barron know about the marriage?

As she walked out of the bathroom, she bumped into Stan. He gave her a smirk too big for his small head. "Now it's Barron Sterling, eh?"

"Back off, Stan." She gritted her teeth at how shaky she sounded. It was galling to look weak in front of the enemy. Stan raised a supercilious eyebrow and walked off; she composed herself and marched back into the conference room.

Barron munched on his sugar cookies, while the partners sat to his left, making small talk and trying to appear nonchalant, as though an associate running out was an everyday occurrence. Vanessa closed the door. "Sorry about that."

"Are you all right? You look a little peaked," Barron said. "Perhaps I shouldn't have barged in like this after the unfortunate incident yesterday, but I simply couldn't wait."

"I'm fine, thank y—"

"I agree with Mr. Sterling." Apparently Barron hadn't given Harry leave to call him by his first name. "You should take some time off. I've seen your billable hours, and you've been working too hard recently. We're all quite concerned."

Concerned? Vanessa's jaw loosened. Harry hated

associates billing fewer than a hundred hours a week, to the point that he called them "parasites." He probably thought she was the most indolent sloth in the history of mankind since she was only working forty.

"Harry's right," Barron said.

"Sir, that's—"

"Vanessa, we're family now. You'll call me Barron, or Uncle Barron, if you wish."

Her hands tightened into fists. "Naturally."

Barron rose to his full height. He wasn't particularly tall, but the confident way he held himself gave him a commanding air. "Take a week or so off. We can do all the right things to welcome you into the family. And perhaps you can change your name while you're at it? Vanessa *Sterling*... It has a certain ring to it."

She forced a smile. "I have to admit, it does," she said, all the while thinking *We'll see.*

HER CELL PHONE WAS RINGING IN HER PURSE WHEN Vanessa made it back to her office. It was Kerri Lloyd, Justin's cousin.

"Oh my gosh, I can't believe you're family now!" Kerri said. "I thought Barron was joking when he told me this morning."

"He wasn't."

"I see that. This is awesome."

"Thank you," Vanessa said through rubbery lips. She stood at her window, not really seeing the view.

There was a beat of silence. "You don't sound so good. Are you still shocked about the accident?"

Vanessa made a non-committal noise.

"We've got to meet and chat. I never pegged Justin for the impulsive elopement type." Then Kerri added, "You either, for that matter. But this is so romantic."

Romantic? "There's nothing to tell, really." It had been about the baby. The heir. Saccharine *I love you*s had never been exchanged.

"You don't expect me to believe that, do you? Listen, I gotta go, but we're definitely meeting up sometime soon. Barron said it was a secret elopement, but now that it's out, I'm sure your parents will want to chat."

Kerri hung up as Vanessa bit back a groan. Damn it. It wasn't just her parents, but her brothers who'd descend upon her. Shane might even call, for news this big.

Two knocks and her door opened. Zoe stuck her head in. "Hey, is it true you're married to Justin Sterling?"

"Where did you hear that?"

"Everyone's talking about it."

She sighed. Apparently, gossip was the only thing in the universe that traveled faster than light. "Yes, it's true."

"Wow. No wonder you almost fainted yesterday." Zoe flushed. "I wish I'd known. I would have phrased things a little differently."

"It wasn't your fault. We were trying to keep it quiet."

"Still, it's so romantic. Young love. Did you elope in Vegas?"

Vanessa shook her head. "Canada."

"Huh. I had no idea Canada was an elopement destination."

"We're just crazy iconoclasts. Um, would you mind closing the door? I have a few things I need to wrap up. And if anybody calls, I'm not in."

"Sure. By the way, Sandra said you have the next two weeks off. She wanted me to remind you."

"Of course," Vanessa said, trying not to kick her desk. Sandra was Harry Dickson's secretary. Harry would've never given her that many days off if she'd asked, but since Barron had practically demanded it… "Thanks."

Vanessa sat down. Her phone rang again, and she turned it off. So many emotions were roiling… and she wanted to throttle Justin for the mess in her office! How could he have let Barron know? Her *husband* had all the finesse of an elephant in heat.

She would've preferred to announce their marriage in a way that would minimize the disruption to both of their lives. Now, with everyone whispering about it everywhere, that was impossible.

Don't be ungrateful. You would've given anything to have Justin alive just a day ago. You got your wish. Don't get angry over something Barron's done. Justin might not have had anything to do with it.

She closed her eyes and dragged in some air. Maybe it would be good for her to take some time off, talk with family, and figure out her next steps. This was just a minor hiccup in her life. Besides the firm was already making it clear she wouldn't have made partner anyway. What did it matter if everyone knew she was a Sterling now? Her career was effectively over.

She turned the phone back on and called Iain and Mark first. Neither picked up—they were generally busy—so she left them both a message, letting them know she was married to Justin Sterling.

Dane, on the other hand, had an assistant who was a news and gossip magnet and superb at reading situations. She instantly connected Vanessa to him.

"Make it short; I'm in a meeting," Dane said.

Vanessa sighed. Work before family—her oldest brother's MO. "I got married."

A stunned silence, then he said, "To whom?"

"Justin Sterling."

"Prenup?"

She frowned. "No."

"You did well then."

"There's more to a marriage than a prenup or lack thereof."

"Of course. But it's nice not to sign one, especially if you're a woman and have fewer assets."

"Do you ever actually listen to yourself?"

"Yes. And as a high-priced lawyer, you know I'm right." He hung up.

She glared at the phone. She should've known Dane would be callous about the whole thing. Not even a token "congratulations."

Well, what did she expect from the manipulative jerk? At least her three other brothers were nice. Since she no longer knew Shane's number, given all his travels, she emailed him a short message, letting him know she was married and that she missed him. It wasn't like Shane to be gone so long, as adventurous as he was.

Then she debated who she should call next. It was going to be either her mom or dad, and she flipped the "inner conflict resolution" quarter she kept in her desk drawer. It came up heads.

She dialed and waited. Ceinlys picked up on the fourth ring. "Hello dear."

"Hi, Mom."

A beat of silence. "What's wrong?"

Vanessa closed her eyes briefly. There was no escaping the maternal mood radar. "I just wanted you to know that I, ah, got married. To Justin."

"You what?"

"I married him. Justin Sterling."

"Justin Sterling."

"Yes."

"When did this happen?"

"About seven weeks ago."

"Vanessa!" Ceinlys gasped. "And you never told me. He didn't mention it either…and both of you came over to my party!"

"Well, we weren't going to tell anybody for the time be—"

"I am not 'anybody.' *Really*, Vanessa. Keeping an affair like this from your own mother. Marrying someone like him isn't just a matter of love."

Ceinlys would know from experience. Vanessa covered her face with a hand.

"Did you negotiate your own prenup?" her mother asked.

She sighed. "There isn't any prenup." Not for a lack of trying. She would've preferred everything to be laid out crystal clear.

Ceinlys made a vague humming noise. "I see. Well. When is the honeymoon?"

"Whenever Barron decides is good, I guess," Vanessa grumbled.

"That man. Don't let him walk all over you. You're family now, not one of the servants."

"Don't worry. By the way, I haven't told this to anybody except Justin, but I'm pregnant."

"Oh." A short pause. "Is that...? Never mind. We should meet and talk about this. Can you get away? I'm in downtown at the moment, and I can be at the Starbucks across from your office in about ten minutes."

"You don't have to change your plans for me," Vanessa said.

"Don't be silly. It's just some shopping."

Ceinlys hung up, and Vanessa stared at her phone. Did she have enough time to talk to her dad? Maybe yes, maybe no. Biting her lip, she dialed his number and sighed with relief when it went to voice mail.

"Dad, I married Justin Sterling about seven weeks ago. I thought I should let you know before Barron calls. Love you, bye."

She picked up her purse and got up, then hesitated. What the heck. She took her briefcase too. She had a feeling she wouldn't be coming back to the office after talking with her mom. It looked like the partners really wanted her to take time off—anything to keep Barron Sterling happy.

There were stares as she left, but she kept her chin up. She would not be cowed by something like this.

Ceinlys had already ordered a drink by the time Vanessa had made it to Starbucks. She got an iced tea and joined her mother at a table in the corner.

Ceinlys was dressed in black slacks topped by a dark magenta silk blouse with a round neck.

Stilettos encased her impeccably pedicured feet, and not a fleck of gray showed in her hair. Her makeup was perfect, her skin smooth and flawless. With diamonds at her ears and throat, she looked like the proverbial million bucks despite going through what had to be a stressful divorce. When people had the kind of assets Ceinlys and Salazar did, divorces rarely were clean and easy… even with a prenup.

Despite her cool disinterest, a few men were checking her out. Vanessa almost bared her teeth at them. Her mother wasn't on display at a meat market.

"So. The baby," Ceinlys said, getting straight to the point.

Vanessa sighed. "Almost eight weeks."

"Is that why you decided to marry?"

"It was mostly his decision. He said something about it's being the heir to the Sterling & Wilson fortune."

"Well, yes, I suppose. But surely, marriage wasn't necessary."

Vanessa took a sip of her tea, which was too bitter. She pushed it aside. "I'm not sure. It's complicated."

"Do you love him?" Ceinlys peered at her.

Vanessa shrugged, then cleared throat. "I don't know. We have…chemistry. We dated when I was in college and law school, then we—actually *I*—broke it off."

"So how did the pregnancy come about?"

Vanessa sighed. "I went to Chicago when I heard about your divorce."

"Ah." A frown creased Ceinlys's forehead briefly. "Do you still want to talk about my divorce?"

"Are you going to tell me to go see Samantha?"

A small smile appeared on her mother's lips. "No. I suppose that wasn't very nice of me. But at the time I didn't want to discuss the matter with anyone who might question my decision."

"Why not?"

"Because it was a very difficult one. And I didn't think I would be able to do what I needed to if people tried to talk me out of it."

"Do you still love him?" Vanessa asked.

Looking away, Ceinlys dragged in a lungful of air and exhaled softly. "In some ways."

"Even though he was so bad to you?"

"We were bad for each other. By the time I realized this, it was too late. There were three children, and I couldn't leave."

Vanessa tapped the table with a fingernail. The infamous Pryce prenup meant her mother would have lost custody of her children, and that wasn't something she would have risked.

"For a time I thought things might change if he realized the prenup had nothing to do with my decision to stay, but…we just weren't meant to be," Ceinlys added.

"Love isn't enough, is it?"

"No." Ceinlys reached over and held Vanessa's hand. "You're a smart girl, so maybe what I'm about to tell you is superfluous, but…" Something in Ceinlys's eyes shifted, grew hard. "Never forget you have to protect yourself. Don't ever let yourself be in a position where you have to depend on somebody else for your happiness and fulfillment in life. Don't ever let emotions cloud your judgment and make you see things that aren't there. I don't want you to have the kind of life that I had. I want you to be free and happy."

Vanessa laid her other hand over her mother's. "Are you free and happy?"

Ceinlys's smile didn't reach her eyes. "Soon, dear. Soon I will be."

SALAZAR DRAINED ANOTHER GLASS OF WHISKEY. The home office was dark except for the light on the desk. It illuminated his mother's portrait. Shirley Pryce had been a harshly beautiful woman with a mind that stayed sharp to the very end. The artist had put a small curve to her lips and softened the lines around her eyes. A complete lie. Shirley Pryce had never smiled easily, and her eyes had always been hard and vigilant.

"You wanted your grandkids to marry well. And gue...guess what? Vanessa snagged Justin Sterling! Can you believe it?" He toasted his mother. "Amazing what that girl can do, eh? Despite your worries about her 'over-education.'"

He staggered over to the liquor cabinet. "S'pose I should call and congratulate Vanessa," he mumbled. "But that would take energy." Ever since Ceinlys had hired Samantha Jones, Salazar hadn't been able to focus on anything.

Why now? He couldn't figure it out. Did she think he'd change his mind about the prenup? Or was it something else?

It was really too bad the best liquors in his cabinet couldn't help him. Because he'd do anything to numb the bitter ball of panic in his gut.

FIFTEEN

His hands still on the keyboard, Justin took another look at his phone. Vanessa hadn't called him back or returned his texts about their weekend getaway to Mexico. Maybe she was occupied doing the busywork her partners had given her. Even though it was clearly bullshit, she dedicated herself to the work, just like always. He appreciated that about her, even though her work ethic could be annoying from time to time.

When his phone rang, he answered immediately. "Justin Sterling."

"Holy shit, you dog!"

He made a face. "Nate?"

"You married Vanessa Pryce? And you didn't tell me when I asked you why you were flying to L.A. so much?"

"*What are you talking about?*" Justin flipped

through all the possibilities in his mind. "Who told you that?"

"Barron. He had his assistant send out a text blast to everyone in the family just now. He said he'd already gone to L.A. personally to welcome her into the family."

His stomach dropped like somebody had disemboweled him. "You've gotta be kidding. When did he go?"

"This morning."

Justin bit back a curse. "How did he find out?"

"Unlike your erstwhile brother, Barron is a suspicious bastard. He probably checked on why you were flying back and forth between San Francisco and L.A. so much. I told you to watch your expenses."

"Damn it." Justin gritted his teeth, thinking *shit shit shit*. "Okay, thanks. Gotta go." He hung up. No wonder Vanessa hadn't contacted him. She was probably furious right now. He tried her number again, but it went to voice mail. He tried the next person on his list.

"How are you doing, Justin? I hear the doctor gave you a clean bill of health, but I don't know if I can trust it."

Justin reined in his temper at the droll tone. "Barron, what did you do?"

"Be more specific. I've done a lot of things in

my life. Actually you can hang up now. I'm right outside your office."

Barron cut the line and simultaneously opened the door to Justin's office. He looked hale and happy, his color high as he walked inside and took an armchair near Justin's desk. "You horrible child. You should've invited me to the wedding."

"Have you considered the possibility that maybe we didn't want to make a big deal about it? That we wanted to keep it to ourselves?"

"Why on earth would you do that?"

"Various reasons." It wasn't really a lie. Vanessa had her big reason, and Justin had the reason of wanting to show support and make her happy. "We were going to keep it quiet until July."

"July! Ridiculous."

A secretary scurried in with a tray of hot tea and sugar cookies. She left it on the table by Barron and ran out as quickly she could.

When the door closed behind her, Justin said, "It may seem ridiculous to you, but not to us. You should've at least talked to me first."

The good humor leeched from Barron's face. "You were unreachable this morning."

"Not on purpose." He'd been on a commercial flight and unable to use his phone.

"I wasn't going to wait. This is about the family."

"No. This is about you trying to show everyone you're still in charge."

"I *am* in charge. I'm the head of this family!"

Justin stared at Barron, who stared right back. *This is it*, Justin thought. If he didn't put his foot down now, Barron would continue to interfere whenever he felt like it. No more. No way. "Then I'm resigning."

"What?" Barron said in a booming voice.

"I quit. If you want to be in charge, you don't need me. I won't play this game, Barron."

"Do you think you're irreplaceable?"

Justin gave him a slight smile. "I wouldn't go that far. Let's say…very difficult to replace. You'll want a family member who'll be okay with attempting to run the company while all the executives try to gauge *your* intentions. But Sterling & Wilson is your legacy, so of course you'll want that person to be trained. And you have Kerri, Nate, Robert, Benjamin and Beatrice to choose from. Thankfully they're all intelligent…it won't be that difficult to mold them."

"You'll be cut off."

"That doesn't bother me."

Barron gave him a penetrating squint. "What's changed? The idea that you might not be my heir always bothered you."

"I found something I value more than Sterling & Wilson."

Barron snorted, then chuckled, the sound reluctant and soft. He reached for his tea. "All this over a girl."

"She's my wife. And she's pregnant."

Barron choked on his tea, and Justin walked over to pound his great-uncle's back with slightly more force than was necessary.

"Pregnant?" Barron gasped. "Are you sure?"

"Yes. About eight weeks now."

A huge grin split Barron's face. "Kerri, and now you!" He let out a booming laugh. "Wonderful!"

"I'm still quitting."

"Don't be ridiculous. Sterling & Wilson is also your son's legacy."

"It may not be a son," Justin pointed out.

"Bah. Son, daughter, what does it matter? Girls can lead a company just as well as boys."

Justin watched his uncle with bemusement. The old curmudgeon sometimes surprised him.

"If it would make you feel better, I suppose I could try to be more considerate of your situation." Barron pursed his lips, but then he noticed the sugar cookies laid out for him. "By the way, did that marketing VP turn in his resignation?"

"Who, Ross?" Justin frowned. "No."

"If he doesn't do so by COB today, fire him."

"Why?"

"He came to me to discuss your comments on his latest ideas yesterday, and I told him to resign."

Justin scowled.

"You have to make examples of a few. Then things will be fine. I won't overrule you no matter who you fire. I'm on the board, but that doesn't mean I want to make managerial decisions. That's your job."

"Fine. I'll talk with Hayashi and see if we can cut the strings on his golden parachute."

Barron smiled. "See? There's a reason I chose you. We always were on the same wavelength, as you youngsters like to say."

After Barron left, Justin got up and stretched, then poured himself a drink. Finally, it looked like he was going to have full control of the company. It was a considerable weight off his shoulders.

As he sipped his scotch he glanced at the clock. It was already a little after one thirty. It was a Friday and victory or no, he didn't feel like staying in the office any longer. Just at that moment a notice came in that there was a replacement jet and pilot waiting for him at the airport.

Okay, time to go to L.A. and do some damage control. But first, he needed to take care of a bit of business.

Rita helped him put away all his documents. "Anything else before you leave?"

"Actually, there is. Can you ask Keith Ross to come to my office?"

"Sure."

"And get the security team ready to escort him out."

Her smile faltered. "Uh… Is he being let go?"

"Yes, but don't tell him. You know the protocol."

She nodded. A few minutes later, Keith showed up. He was always well-packaged—an expensive suit, an expensive watch and expensive shoes. His dark hair was slicked back, the high forehead shiny as a pebble in a river. "Hey, boss. You wanted to see me?"

"Yes. Close the door." Justin pointed his chin at the armchair and waited until the other man was seated. "You're being let go effective immediately."

His eyes bulged out, making him look like a goldfish. "*What?*"

"You heard me."

"Why? My performance has been exemplary."

"If you truly believe that, you're delusional. Your performance has been adequate, but is outweighed by your disruptive influence. Nobody can undermine my authority and expect to stay on my team."

"Jesus." He raked a hand through his hair. "Is this because I called Barron yesterday?"

Justin merely sat back and watched Keith's face turn red.

"It was just to get some feedback. It wasn't like I was going over your head."

"Spin, spin, spin," Justin said, circling his finger in the air.

"Come on! I have a family."

"Then you should've done your job, which doesn't include running to Barron every time you disagree with my decisions. *I* sit in the CEO's seat. *I* call the shots."

"Justin—"

"I've been lenient with you, but obviously that hasn't worked. Security will escort you out." Justin got up and left, while the former VP sputtered. Outside his office two large men dressed in black were waiting.

That taken care of, he called Mark Pryce to make a reservation at his restaurant. They should probably do a big family dinner with Vanessa's relatives since none of them had gotten invited to the wedding. Then he groaned when he saw a call from his mother. Ever since his father passed away, she'd lived like a hermit, but for her to call was serious. There was no way to avoid this one.

"Hi, Mom!" he said extra cheerily.

"Justin Augustine Sterling!"

He winced. She hadn't used his full name or that tone of voice since he was twelve.

"I cannot *believe* you got married and didn't tell me about it!"

He didn't mention she wouldn't have come to the ceremony anyway since she didn't like to travel, and a small town in Ohio was probably not a suitable venue for an overpriced high society wedding. "I didn't invite Barron either," he said lamely.

"He's your great-uncle. I'm your *mother!*"

"I know, I know. Look, I'm sorry. But don't worry. I married a very nice, very smart girl. Vanessa Pryce. You remember her, right?" His mother might not get out much, but she didn't live in a bunker either.

There was a pause. "Yes. The lawyer girl?"

"Right."

"I thought you were dating London."

"Well…I was. It didn't work out."

"And that was only a few weeks ago. How is it that you suddenly changed your mind and fell in love with Vanessa?"

Justin smiled at how outraged his mother sounded.

"Please don't tell me you married her because of her looks. Vanessa's a nice girl, but I'm afraid you might have gone for the looks. I've yet to see a girl that gorgeous, except possibly for the Fairchild girl." Catherine Fairchild was so good-looking, she didn't even seem human at times.

"Don't worry, Mom. I didn't marry her for looks. We've been dating on and off since college. You remember how I went to Stanford, even though Barron wanted me to go to Harvard?"

"Yes. You argued quite a bit over that, as I recall."

"Vanessa was attending Stanford Law."

"Oh."

"As much as I love a pretty face, I also enjoy good conversation."

She sighed. "I suppose I ought to have more faith, but it's so difficult. Barron gave you too much of *everything* too soon. It's just not normal for a young man to grow up the way you did and not lose some sense of proportion. I never like how he kept pushing you to be as horrible and entitled as possible."

He chuckled. It was no secret she disapproved of Barron's Machiavellian ways. "Don't worry, Mom. I haven't forgotten anything you taught me."

"Good. But you're going to bring her home soon? I want to see her."

"We'll have to see our schedule. She's pretty busy. Besides, she's pregnant."

"Already?" There was a pause. "Did she get pregnant before or after you married her?"

"I...don't know. It happened so fast."

"I suppose it doesn't really matter." She let out something that sounded suspiciously like a squeal. "Oh my stars, I'm going to be a grandmother!"

"Looks like it."

"All right then. You bring her home soon. And

let me know if she's allergic to anything. I'm going to cook."

Justin smiled at that. His mother rarely cooked these days, but when she did it was a treat. "All right. Will do. Love you, Mom."

"Love you too. I hope you two make each other as happy as your father made me."

SIXTEEN

By the time Vanessa arrived home a little after five, Justin was waiting for her. She gave him a hard look. "I can't believe you did what you did."

He put his hands up, palms out. "Hey, I didn't tell anyone. Barron found out."

"How? We were in a helicopter, and our witnesses were your lawyers. Did they talk?"

"No. It's my fault. He noticed expenses related to my commute and decided to dig around."

"*Expenses?* Since when does the world's fifth richest man worry about expenses?"

"I know. But Barron's suspicious. He didn't grow up rich, so he checks everything. I should've anticipated that and done things differently." Justin made a face. "Was he bad?"

"You would *not* believe! He forced two weeks' vacation on me. He insisted I be welcomed 'properly' into the family without consulting me on the timing or anything. No, it's what he wants, so that's the way it's going to happen." Vanessa stopped to take a breath. "FYI, Mom knows about the baby. There was no way I could keep quiet about us once Barron visited the office. Then of course Mom wanted to know why we married, so I had to tell her."

"That's fine. Your mom has every right to worry."

Vanessa nodded, not telling him about the rest of the conversation. Her mother had always wanted her to protect herself, and she knew that was the smart thing to do. She was comfortable, but didn't have as much money as people assumed, since after having taken her inheritance to buy the condo and pay off her debts, she'd spent most of it setting up a nationwide non-profit organization, Just and Proper Help, to provide legal aid to the poor. The only person who knew she was behind it was Gavin Lloyd, and that was only because he managed its assets. She'd never had the time to really get involved in running the NPO, and she preferred to keep her connection to it quiet.

"We have a reservation at Éternité tonight," Justin said. "Mark and Iain will be joining us, probably with their fiancées."

Ah, okay. That explained why her brothers hadn't called yet. They were probably saving all their questions for the face-to-face inquisition. At least

Justin would be there to help her handle them. *I should get my rings from the jewelry box for dinner.* There was no reason to keep them hidden anymore.

"I'm not sure about Dane, though. I just left a message with his assistant. And I invited your parents as well."

She looked up quickly. "Both of them?"

"Yes. I thought about doing it separately, but each asked me to invite the other."

Vanessa frowned. She'd been certain they wouldn't want to be anywhere near each other. Maybe they just didn't want to be jerks in front of the new Sterling son-in-law. Getting Justin was a coup by anyone's standards, and if her grandmother had been alive, she would've praised Vanessa to the skies. "By the way, Kerri called. I think we may have to do an obligatory dinner or something soon with your side of the family, too."

"No, we don't, not unless you want to."

She shook her head. "The cat's out of the bag, so we should do what's expected of us. I don't want any friction, especially right off the bat." She knew what that was like at home with her family, all the tension and unspoken words on every holiday. It would be nice to avoid that, not just for her sake, but for the sake of their child. She didn't particularly look forward to holidays, but she wanted her children to anticipate every one of them with joy.

“Okay. I’ll take care of it. And let Rita know when your next doctor’s appointment is so she can put that on my calendar.”

“Aren’t you going to be busy?” The accident from the day before must’ve screwed up his schedule for the next few weeks.

“I’m always busy.” He put a warm, strong hand over her belly. “But you and the baby matter more.”

She blinked away sudden tears. She didn’t know why she felt like crying just now when he was being so sweet. It had to be hormones.

Or maybe she was just scared he was becoming too irresistible for her own good. She could put up a shield against thoughtless gestures and harsh words, but what protection was there against such sweetness when all she wanted to do was sink into it? It spun seductive images of their future, each one a giant wave of warmth and happiness washing over the dark frissons of her doubts.

She put her arms around him and buried her face in his chest. Then wished fervently that what they had would never change.

Éternité was packed by the time Vanessa and Justin arrived. It was an interesting melding of French and Japanese sensibilities. The transparent hangings with hand-embroidered designs swirling like flags from the high ceiling reflected the meeting of east and west. Justin had never been to the restaurant, but he assumed it would be excellent—after all, it was Mark's.

The tuxedoed maître d' led them to a private party room on the second level. Justin's mouth watered at the scent of seared meat and seafood and butter and sauces. He hadn't realized he was quite that hungry. He turned to Vanessa. "Are you feeling okay? No nausea or anything?"

"I'm fine."

He squeezed her gently, and they went in to meet their dinner companions.

Her brothers, Iain and Mark, were both dark with what everyone called the classic Pryce profile—clean and aristocratic, with a high forehead and a patrician angle to the bridge of the nose. Nobody looking at them would have ever questioned the family connection. Justin noted Iain's slightly narrowed eyes. His friend was probably feeling conflicted right now. He was quite protective of his siblings, since Dane, the oldest Pryce brother, was somewhat of a jerk. Justin considered Iain the "good cop" of the two, while Mark was just laid back.

As predicted, they'd also brought their fiancées. Next to Iain was a brunette with a shy smile who must be Jane Connolly. *How surprising*. Justin had always thought his friend would end up with a flashy model named after a fruit. Mark had come with Hilary Rosenberg, whom Justin was familiar with already. He and her boss were related by marriage.

Hilary and Jane rose and hugged Vanessa, then Hilary introduced Jane and Justin, while the Pryce men greeted their sister.

"Where are your folks?" Justin asked.

"They're both running late," Mark said. "Just called a few minutes ago. Separately, of course. We better talk before they show."

Justin quirked an eyebrow. Surely Salazar and Ceinlys could be civilized for something like this, even if it came during their divorce. After all, they'd been civilized while they were married, and their relationship had been nothing more than a wedded farce.

Iain turned to Vanessa. "Tell me how this came about."

"How it came about? We eloped. What's there to say?"

Mark snorted. "You're not the eloping type." He opened the menu and perused it. A superfluous gesture. Mark probably knew every item by heart. "Don't get the special," he said.

"Why not?" Justin asked, eyeing the tuna.

"Specials generally mean 'old but not yet bad' stuff we're trying to unload. The lobsters are good today," Mark said.

And most likely the most expensive item. The

menu didn't have prices on it, but Justin could play this. "Then we'll have lobsters."

"An excellent choice!" Jane said. "André is a genius with lobsters."

"Didn't you say that about him and lamb last time?" Iain asked.

She looked up at him adoringly. "He's a genius with anything related to food."

Justin watched the lovebirds in front of him chatting and smiling. There was something about them that made his chest ache. Maybe it was the total intimacy and easy way the couples interacted. Justin didn't know how long they'd been together, but it couldn't have been more than a few months.

He wished he and Vanessa had the same kind of easy rapport, but things had been tense between them for the past few months. Right now she was staring at the menu without really reading anything. "What's wrong?" he whispered. "Don't you see anything you like?"

"No. I'm sure everything's great."

A sheen of sweat glistened along her hairline. "Too warm in here?" Justin asked, but she shook her head.

"So, tell us how he proposed," Hilary said. "I think it's awesome that you couldn't wait to get married. So romantic."

"We can elope if you want," Mark said, and she slapped his arm with a laugh.

"I proposed on my plane. With that ring right there."

Vanessa tilted her hand so everyone could see it.

"So simple but so elegant," Hilary breathed.

"Classy," Jane said. "I love it." She smiled at Justin. "You have great taste."

"True," Justin said. "I—"

Vanessa bolted to her feet, her face paper-white.

"What's wrong?" Mark asked.

She ran out.

Hilary watched the direction Vanessa was running toward, then said, "Oh."

"What?" Mark said.

She turned to Justin. "She's pregnant. Isn't she?"

No way to hide it now. Justin nodded.

She got up. "I'll go see if she needs any help."

"How far along is she?" Jane asked as Hilary left.

"About eight weeks, I guess."

"Son of a bitch," Iain muttered, and she put a hand on his sleeve. He glared at Justin. "I asked you to watch my sister, and you got her pregnant instead?" Then he stopped. "Wait, is that why she married you? Because you guys had a one-night stand and she felt like she had to get married or something?"

"For your information, we've never had one-night stand. We've been dating since she was in college and law school."

Iain and Mark stared like he'd just told them Martians had landed in West Hollywood.

"*Ten years?* No way. We would've known about it," Iain said.

"No offense, man, but you need better intel."

"So what happened after law school?" Iain demanded.

Justin shrugged. How much to tell his irate friend? "We sort of went our separate ways, with her in L.A. and me in various cities for Sterling & Wilson. Sometimes we saw each other when it made sense."

"I can't believe I'm hearing this. You had, like, a decade of booty calls with my sister?"

"Uh, I wouldn't put it quite that way."

Jane cleared her throat. "Iain, if Vanessa didn't want to marry him, she wouldn't have. It's not like she lacks options."

"Yeah, yeah, you're right," Iain said. "But that doesn't mean I'm okay with it." He scowled at Justin. "Do you love her?"

Did he? Justin wanted her and wanted to spoil her and spend his life with her, but he wasn't sure if it was the same thing as the kind of love Iain wanted to hear. Besides, he hadn't even told Vanessa he loved her, and he wasn't going to tell Iain anything first. So he merely cocked an eyebrow. "Why else would I have married her? I could've always just offered to pay child support instead."

"And I would've kicked your ass," Iain said.

Vanessa came back with Hilary. Her face was flushed, but otherwise she looked all right. "What are you guys talking about?" she asked, taking her seat next to Justin.

"Whether or not to kill Justin," Iain said at the same time Mark said, "Dinner." Mark signaled the waiter, and two baskets of warm bread appeared on the table. "You know it's been a while since we had a big family dinner. Can we try to have a good one?"

"I second that motion," Hilary said.

Jane raised a hand. "Third!"

Everyone started ordering, much to Justin's relief.

Then Salazar showed up, and Ceinlys a few moments later.

The last time Justin had seen Salazar was at his cousin Kerri's wedding. There, the older man had been robust and glowing with health and alcohol. He was still dashing in his carefully tailored clothes; silver touched the temples of his black hair just so to hint at worldliness without suggesting advanced age, and his well-cared for skin was a light bronze. But there was a dullness to him now, like a hazy film over glass.

Ceinlys, on the other hand, looked much the same as before—wealthy, elegant, with just a hint of superiority. Ironically enough, the latter reminded Justin of Shirley Pryce, Ceinlys's great adversary.

They sat at opposite ends of the table without any prompting. Salazar didn't even glance at the menu. "Just bring me the most expensive item and a shot of whiskey," he said, then turned to Justin. "So. Married."

Justin nodded.

Salazar's mouth smiled. "May you two be happy."

"I can't imagine why they wouldn't," Ceinlys said, not looking up from the menu. Her tone had the ponderousness of an English lit professor pontificating on the meaning of "nunnery" from Hamlet's monologue. She finally folded the leather folio closed. "You should have a real ceremony for family and friends."

"The original one they had was real enough." Salazar downed the shot of whiskey and gestured for another. "Unless you're implying it's fake?"

"No more fake than ours." Ceinlys gave him a precise smile, but her eyes stayed cold.

Salazar held her gaze, while his children reached for more bread. "If you want a ceremony, you can pay for it."

"I'm sure that won't be necessary. Barron undoubtedly wants one as well."

A waiter brought a glass of champagne for her, breaking the exchange. Justin leaned over. "Is it always like this?" he whispered to Vanessa.

"Actually they're behaving pretty well."

His jaw slackened. If this was the good version, he couldn't imagine how bad the regular one was. He'd assumed the family dinner would be semi-friendly since it was really about Vanessa and his marriage, not Salazar and Ceinlys's situation. Tension crept into the back of his neck and shoulders as Salazar and Ceinlys kept sniping at each other.

Vanessa put a hand over his wrist. "Relax. Just pretend you're not here, and you should be all right."

"Sorry. I should've never invited them."

"They're the parents, so we would've had to eat with them at some point. It's fine. Really." She flashed him a quick smile.

He squeezed her hand. "I can't believe you're trying to cheer me up."

She shrugged. "I'm used to this."

His phone buzzed, and he glanced at it. It was a text from Dane.

Can't make it. You're an idiot for inviting both my parents. If you make Vanessa unhappy, I'll kill you. Anything else we can discuss later.

Mentally shaking his head, Justin typed: *Appreciate the congrats.* He hesitated, then decided the rest of what he wanted to say needed to be said in person.

A few seconds later came a response: *You're welcome.*

The food smelled amazing, but he couldn't remember what it was or how it tasted. All he could feel was the hostility under the glittery civilized veneer that Vanessa's parents projected and the silent tension as the rest of them went through the motions of dining. By the time they reached the fish course, he couldn't eat anything without feeling like there was a drill in his gut, and Vanessa hadn't touched much of anything except some bread.

Justin had heard rumors about how awkward Pryce family dinners could be, but this was worse than he'd imagined. No wonder Dane hadn't bothered to show. Justin felt like an idiot for having arranged the event in the first place.

At the same time he was beginning to see why Vanessa was so skittish about marriage, commitment and family. She had no role model, nothing she could emulate or aspire to.

He ached for her and wished he could replace all her bad memories with good ones.

SEVENTEEN

Dinner hadn't gone as badly as Vanessa had feared, all things considered. She'd already expected her parents to be unhappy, so that hadn't been surprising. But Justin, normally relaxed in situations where others would freeze up, had been so tense the whole time she felt awful for him.

As they waited for the valet to bring out their cars, Iain pulled her aside. "So you're really happy?" he asked.

She nodded.

"You know you can come to me any time there's a problem, right? I'm always here, always got your back. Don't let Justin intimidate you."

"Do I look like the 'easy to intimidate' type?"

"You don't know him the way I do. He looks all nice and cool, but if you're in the way of what he wants, he has no problem crushing you. He learned from the best."

True. Barron Sterling had a terrible reputation in that regard. "I can handle Justin. And if I need help, I have your number."

"Good." He gave her an extra-tight hug. "There's my car. Talk to you soon?"

She nodded and watched her brother leave with Jane. Then her mother came out—sans Salazar—and strode toward her rapidly.

"Oh, good you're still here." She gave Justin a quick smile. "Do you mind? I need to steal Vanessa for a moment."

Ceinlys led Vanessa off a small distance and lowered her voice. "We already spoke about your marriage, so I won't repeat what I said. Something occurred to me just now, and I thought you should be aware."

"What is it?"

"I've been getting some odd calls. You probably will too."

"What do you mean?"

"You just married one of the wealthiest and most influential men in the world. People will try to use you to get to him."

Vanessa gaped at Ceinlys. "Seriously? Do we know anybody that crass?"

Ceinlys sighed. "It is simply impossible to underestimate some people's behavior. Anyway, I need to say good-bye to Mark and Hilary. I just rushed out to catch you." She gave Vanessa two air kisses, waved at Justin and slipped back into the restaurant.

Vanessa walked slowly back to Justin, who put an arm around her. "Your family has a lot of secrets."

"They're just worried."

"I will make you happy."

A small pang in her heart. Not because she didn't think he was lying, but she didn't think he realized how empty such promises were at the end of the day. Would he believe her if she told him her father had vowed the same to her mother? And just look at how the dinner had just turned out. "I don't think that's what they're worried about."

Finally the valet brought out Justin's car. Just as she was about to walk inside, she stopped.

"What is it?" Justin said. "Do you feel sick again?"

"No." She leaned forward, staring at a couple walking up the street toward them. The man's hand rested against the small of his companion's back, and the woman looked extremely familiar. As they passed under the light, her face was illuminated, and Vanessa gasped.

Justin looked at the couple. "Do you know them?"

"Yes. That's Ginger Maxwell!"

"Ah…who?"

"Shane's fiancée!"

Ginger was laughing at something the man said, her head tilted toward him in a comfortable, intimate way. Vanessa couldn't believe this. How dare she!

Without even thinking, Vanessa ran down the street after them. She felt Justin follow.

"Hey!" Vanessa said. "You cheating scum!"

The man turned and stared. "Do I know you?"

"Not you. Her!" She pointed at Ginger.

The small blonde gaped. "Vanessa?"

"I would've never believed this if I hadn't seen it with my own eyes. What the hell?"

The shock vanished from Ginger's face. She put a hand on her hip. "Do you *mind?* I'm trying to have a nice evening out with my date here."

"Oh my god, are you serious? You're engaged to my brother!"

"I'm completely *not* engaged to your dickhead of a brother. He dumped me five months ago." She turned to her date. "Really, I'm not engaged to anyone. I swear."

Vanessa's jaw slackened. "What? How… He contacted you?"

"No, like an idiot I went to see him. After I didn't hear from him for weeks, I might add." Something dark and painful flickered in her eyes, then died as she tightened her fists. "I'd waited since forever, and he acted like he didn't even *know* me!

So I'm moving on, because you know what? Shane's not the only man out there." Ginger linked fingers with her date. "Now if you're just *all done* jumping to conclusions, we have a movie to catch." They turned and walked off.

Justin put a hand on her shoulder. "You okay?"

Vanessa stared after the two. "I don't get it." Her mind felt blank. "They were so in love." Was love not enough after all?

"Sometimes couples break up."

"But with the love of their lives?"

"Maybe it wasn't really the love of their lives."

"No, no. Shane and Ginger were together since *high school*."

"Well…feelings change."

Like her parents. All those passionate love letters, but the love had turned into poison and they were now divorcing. Logically, she knew it was better than staying together and being miserable. You didn't have to be alone to feel lonely. But emotionally…

Her mother's words came back to her. *Love wasn't enough*. And children certainly weren't enough to keep a couple together. They were often pawns used to squeeze more concessions out of the other party.

Vanessa's marriage didn't even have love as the foundation. They were together for the baby, but would that be enough for them in later years? Or would Justin resent the fact that her pregnancy had trapped him into doing the right thing?

"I'm sure there's more to the story than just her version," Justin was saying. "We won't know the whole truth until Shane gets back."

The ring on her finger flashed, and she looked at the brilliant diamond, the sapphires…this supposed symbol of his commitment to her. But was it? Unlike most men, Justin could buy millions of those rings without a second thought. It was about as significant as a lollipop she'd received from a boy in kindergarten.

Suddenly cold, Vanessa hugged herself.

EIGHTEEN

VANESSA WENT TO A MID-MORNING CLASS at the yoga studio. She was restless, and hoped some exercise would help her regain some balance. The previous night had been awful, full of crazy, vivid nightmares about her being trapped. She'd been as small as a cricket, and a clear glass jar had been put over her. She punched and kicked it, but it didn't even crack. Then as panic grew in her chest, she saw a gigantic Justin outside. He had a forefinger on the jar, and he was staring at her with a smug smile. "Gotcha."

"Where's my family?" she'd yelled, but it had been no use.

Dane, Shane, Iain and Mark wagged their fingers at her, and then Ginger was there. She put her hand on the back of Justin's head and kissed him deeply, and he kissed her back.

Vanessa shook her head to clear her mind. It was just a bad dream, a mix of her anxiety and Ginger.

A petite brunette walked up. "Hey," she said.

There was an instant of non-recognition, then the name clicked. "Hi, Peggy."

"You here alone?"

"Yeah. Just me today."

"Oh." Peggy cleared her throat, her cheeks pinkening. "Do you mind if we talk privately for a moment before class?"

Vanessa checked the time. They had at least fifteen minutes before it started. "Sure."

The two women went to a green juice and smoothie bar adjacent to the studio. It served freshly made spinach and kale concoctions that Vanessa loved for the quick and easy micronutrient effect. It seemed more natural than taking a bunch of pills. "So."

"Um." Peggy's left foot started tapping rapidly. Vanessa glanced down at it, but Peggy seemed oblivious. "I… I didn't really come here for a job. I actually came to L.A. to see you. I called your law firm to see you, but they said you weren't available to take on any new clients and hung up on me."

Vanessa sighed and shot her an apologetic smile. "I'm sorry they treated you that way. I've been sort of"—she struggled for the right word—"busy with things."

"I know. I heard you're an amazing lawyer."

With a career that was going nowhere fast. "If you want, I can give you some referrals."

"Oh, no, please." Peggy waved away. "I wanted to talk to *you*."

"Okay, sure."

"It's just…I don't know how to begin, but we're sisters."

"We're… I'm sorry, what?"

"We're sisters. Half-sisters, really."

Vanessa's mind blanked for a moment, then heat flooded her face. Was Peggy another of Salazar's love children? She didn't look anything like him, but it was entirely possible, given the number of mistresses her father had had. "Um. Okay… You're sure about this?"

"One hundred percent. But I'm happy to take a test or whatever if you want." Peggy shifted. "Look, I'm not here to ask anything for myself, but…the fact is, my mom has cancer, and neither one of us can afford the chemo. I was wondering if there's any way you can help with the cost. I know it's a lot to ask, but…" Peggy blinked fast, dropping her gaze. "I don't know what else to do. I tried not to involve you, but it's been impossible. It's just… totally shameless of me to ask, but could you please do this for me? Save my mom? She's all I have."

Sighing, Vanessa pressed her temples. It would've been more logical for Peggy to approach

Salazar, but he wasn't an easy man to get to with his wall of lawyers and assistants. "I'll see what I can do." He'd given his other illegitimate child, Blaine, fifty million bucks. Vanessa didn't see why he wouldn't be as generous with his daughter.

Still, this would hurt Ceinlys. Vanessa remembered how furious her mother had been when Salazar had claimed Blaine as his own. Couldn't her father have been more careful? Or maybe her mother would be happy this time, since it would strengthen her position in the divorce proceedings.

Peggy visibly sagged. "Thank you."

"How can I get in touch with you?"

"Here." Peggy jotted down ten digits on a napkin and handed it to Vanessa. "Thank you, thank you, thank you."

"Don't thank me yet. I haven't done anything." Vanessa sucked down the rest of her smoothie and went outside. She had zero desire to exercise now.

She hopped into her car and drove to the family mansion. Her father lived there alone now, along with staff who kept the place clean and habitable. She'd always thought the place was somewhat ostentatious, but it'd been in the family for generations, and her family wasn't going to give it up just because she didn't care for it.

Al, impeccably dressed as always, welcomed her. The butler had been a standard fixture at her house ever since she could remember. "Miss."

"Is dad home?"

He nodded. "In his study."

She went to the second level. The study was large, with big windows, and held hundreds of books that nobody had read. Her grandmother, Shirley Pryce, had hated it when people touched them. One pale green wall had portraits of the Pryce grandparents.

Salazar was in a plushy armchair. The smile from the previous evening was gone, along with the sparkle in his eyes. His shoulders were slumped, his face slack like the skin was about to slide off it. The usual crispness of his clothes was gone, leaving him looking…sloppy. He was Dorian Gray after the mirror had broken, showing every year of his age.

Vanessa swallowed a gasp. How could he have changed so quickly? If she hadn't known how arrogant and proud he could be, she might have suggested he go see a doctor.

"Congratulations on your marriage," he said without getting up. A small smile ghosted on his lips. "Realized I wasn't cheery enough yesterday. Justin Sterling is quite a catch."

"He is, but the 'catch' factor isn't why I married him."

"Right, right. I heard you're pregnant. He had to do the right thing. Barron would've disowned him otherwise."

Ignoring the jab, Vanessa sat on a couch perpendicular to his chair. "Dad, is there something you want to announce to the family?"

He frowned. "Like what?"

She sighed. "Have you been getting calls from a woman named Peggy?"

"Not that I know of, but Kim handles those things."

Breathing deeply, Vanessa gave herself time to prep what she was about to say. "I saw your daughter today."

He squinted, some of his usual sharpness coming back. "What?"

"Yep. Came up to me in yoga class, introduced herself as my half-sister. She said her mother's sick with cancer. She wanted to know if I could help out."

"She's lying. If she approaches you again, call the police."

Vanessa gasped. "How can you say that? Her mother's your former lover."

"*If* I ever slept with her, which I doubt. Where is she from and what's her mother's name?"

"Her name's Peggy Teeter, and I don't know her mother's name. But she's from Provo, Utah." This was probably futile. According to gossip, Salazar had lovers in every city in the country.

"I don't recall ever sleeping with anyone named Teeter, and I never took a lover in Provo. Just because I have a reputation doesn't mean I'm not discriminating." He gave an offhand flick of his fingers. "Uptight religious girls aren't really my thing."

"So it's just that simple to you?" Outrage suddenly seared through her. "I've never seen you act this cold toward women before. Are you worried about being responsible for the cancer treatment or is it something else?" She shook her head before he could answer. "No, wait. You want to deny everything, so you'll look better in the court of public opinion and Mom won't have as strong a case. Is that it?"

Suddenly Salazar blinked. "Wait, did you say Provo? And this woman claims she's your sister?"

"Yes."

"Not my daughter? Just your sister?"

Now that she thought about it, Peggy actually hadn't said anything about Salazar. "Yes, but—"

He laughed. The sound was nasty but some animation came back to his face. "Oh, this is good."

The sudden change in demeanor was startling. "What?" she said warily. "What's good?"

Salazar shook his head mirthfully, wiping his eyes. "Well, honey, the fact is, you're not related to this Peggy through me. You're related through your mother."

"Through…mom?"

"Oh yes. Peggy's father was one of your mother's boy toys."

Vanessa's jaw loosened, and her thoughts scattered. "Mom had a baby with another man?" But how could Ceinlys have hidden it? Peggy looked to be about Vanessa's age.

A look of half regret and half pain passed through Salazar's face. "Your mother had an affair, found herself pregnant and seduced me so she could pass the child off as mine. Except I knew it wasn't."

"How," she whispered. "How could you be so sure?"

Salazar looked at her levelly. "Because I had a vasectomy right after Shane was born."

Right after… Vanessa felt like somebody had punched her in the stomach, forgetting all about Peggy. An icy fist gripped her heart. "You're lying."

"'Fraid not."

"But…why didn't you let everyone know I'm not yours? It would've been so easy."

"Ah, I didn't want to make a big deal about it. What's one extra mouth to feed?"

Her eyes burned. "Dad…" she whispered, but her voice was so low, she didn't know if he heard her. She couldn't breathe. *One extra mouth to feed.* Was that all she was to him?

"Don't look at me like that. I've always been fair to you. If you want to know about your biological father, you'll have to talk to Ceinlys. And I'd prefer that you didn't advertise the fact that you aren't mine. That would be embarrassing to your mother."

"And to you."

He shook his head. "Men have more leeway. Call it unfair all you want, but that's the way society works. Ceinlys would be judged."

"Why would you care?"

"Until the divorce is finalized, she's still my wife. And my wife is my concern."

She started shaking. How could her father sit there and talk in such a calm tone? "If Mom is really your concern, why did you hurt her by having affairs? Why did you stop loving her? You said you loved her when you proposed. You sent her hundreds of love letters and dried rose petals."

All the warmth and humor left Salazar's face. He looked as unyielding as a statue. "Because she hurt me first. She betrayed my love. The only thing she loved about me was my money. So she got it. But nothing beyond that, because she didn't deserve it. Do you know what it's like to sleep with a woman, knowing all the while she doesn't want you?" His voice gained volume. "No, you wouldn't. Because you're young and stupid and idealistic and you think people only have sex for love or some such ridiculous reason. Listen very carefully, Vanessa. People have sex because it's useful. It's a tool you can use to cut or soothe, depending on your mood, and every time I had sex with your mother it cut me to the core. So I started having sex with other women to cut her back." Suddenly he clicked his teeth shut and glared at her like it was her fault he'd said so much. "Out. *Now!*"

When she didn't move fast enough to suit him, he threw a glass. It exploded against the wall behind her.

"*Get out!*" Veins stood in stark relief on his forehead.

Vanessa jumped to her feet and rushed out. She couldn't believe what she'd heard. This had to be a horrible dream. She just hadn't woken up yet. Soon her alarm would go off, Justin would smile at her, and she'd laugh at how crazy her subconscious mind could be.

Her feet tangled, and she fell forward, landing on her palms in the hallway.

Al rushed up the stairs, his normally impassive face pale. "Miss, are you all right?"

Nausea that had nothing to do with morning sickness rolled through her. Dragging in air seemed impossible with the tight vise around her chest. She croaked, "Bathroom."

He reached down and helped her up. They reached a small guest bathroom, and she threw up her breakfast. Her gut continued to clench and unclench like it wanted to expel every morsel, every drop. Even when nothing was left, her body kept spasming. Closing her eyes, she wished she could get rid of her shock and misery as easily as the food she'd had.

Finally she fell back on her heels, her head lolling listlessly against the cold tiled wall. Her insides felt like somebody had raked them clean. She crawled to the sink and gripped the porcelain edge, pulling herself up. Then very slowly, she flushed the toilet and cleaned herself up. The mirror showed her an awful reflection. Red blotches mottled her pale face, and tendrils of hair hung limp with sweat and water.

A small glass of ginger ale appeared in her vision. "This should help," Al said.

"Thanks," she said hoarsely. She took a small sip of the cold, sweet drink. Her throat hurt too much to finish it. "I'd like to go home. And if you heard anything, don't tell anybody. I'll deal with it later." She had no idea what she was going to say about the news.

"Of course." He glanced down at her still unsteady legs. "Would you like me to help you to your car?"

"Please."

He escorted her down the stairs, his hands on her elbow and at the small of her back. She was grateful for the support. She didn't think she could've made it on her own.

She climbed into her car. Her hands were trembling so badly, it took her a couple of tries to start the engine.

Salazar—dad—*isn't my dad after all.* And she wasn't who she'd thought she was all her life.

Her parents hated each other, used sex to hurt each other. All the love they'd professed for each other had been a big fat joke, lies spun to lead them on the most miserable path imaginable.

No wonder her father had seemed preoccupied whenever he was dealing with her. He probably wondered about the other man every time he looked at her.

Hot tears streamed down her cheeks and wet her shirt. She'd never suspected her parents' marriage was something this foul. And never once did she expect to see her father lose control like that. Her father embodied cool, easy charm. Nothing…absolutely nothing had been able to ruffle his feathers.

Vanessa put her hands on the steering wheel, but she was too shaky to drive. Her legs felt stiff and heavy, and there was no way she could drive back to her condo in her condition.

She managed to pull out her phone and speed-dial Justin. "Can you come get me?" she asked as soon as he answered.

"What's wrong?" His voice was tight. "Where are you?"

"Outside my parents' house. Hurry."

Justin cursed. Vanessa sounded awful, her voice thin and weak. He'd never heard her like that before. What had happened to her? And why was she at her parents' place instead of the yoga studio?

He wasn't familiar with L.A., but by taking directions over the phone as he drove he was able to reach the Pryces' place within an hour. She was slumped over the steering wheel. He got out of his car and knocked on the window. "Hey."

She raised her head. He gaped at how wretched she looked. Her eyes and nose were red, and tears glistened on her cheeks and chin. Her misery was a kick to his gut, and he opened the door.

"Sweetheart…what's wrong?"

He got the seatbelt out of the way and wrapped his arms around her. Her control seemed precarious, so he simply cradled her head on his shoulder for the moment. Tremors ran through her; he whispered soothing nothings as he stroked her back.

A man who had to be Salazar's butler appeared.

"What happened?" Justin demanded, starting to stand up.

"No." Vanessa put a hand on his chest. "I just want to go home. Please?"

It was an effort not to grab the butler and start shaking answers out of him, but Justin took a rough breath and nodded. He grabbed her keys, purse and other items. "I'll send somebody for the car."

"That isn't strictly necessary, sir," the man said. "I can have it driven to her condo this afternoon if you'll leave me the keys."

Justin nodded in agreement. That would be easier. He didn't want to leave Vanessa even for a moment.

She sat in the passenger seat, letting Justin take care of every detail. That more than anything else worried him. Vanessa was normally far too independent to just let people do things for her.

Her eyes were closed the entire time he drove, but he knew she wasn't asleep. The sound of her breathing was erratic, and every so often she'd wipe at her eyes.

When they reached the condo, he made some hot lemon tea and handed it to her. She took a few sips, leaning against the kitchen counter. Then wordlessly, she put the mug down and went to the bedroom, shoulders slumped and feet dragging. She barely managed to kick off her shoes before she fell on the bed and curled up, hugging a pillow. Justin spooned her, breathing in the soft scent of her shampoo and sweat.

The part of him that went out and fixed things wanted to grill her until she told him everything. Then he would know what to do. But the empathetic part could see that whatever had happened must've been pretty traumatic, and so it would be better to wait until she was ready to talk.

One thing he knew: whoever had hurt her was going to pay. People always said it was Barron who had no sense of proportion, that he was the meanest and most vengeful son of a bitch on the planet. They had no idea. Justin hadn't just learned from the old man, he'd surpassed him. Just because he kept his claws and fangs hidden didn't mean they weren't there.

"I met…my half-sister," Vanessa said finally.

He frowned. It was no secret her family had a half-brother named Blaine, who was Salazar's by-blow with some woman in Tennessee. "Blaine has a sister? I thought he was an only ch—"

"No. It's not Salazar's. It's"—she inhaled and exhaled—"hers. My *mom's*."

Justin looked up at the ceiling, thinking *Uh oh…*

"Her name's Peggy. My new half-sister."

He'd always known Ceinlys had lovers. Not that he'd ever blamed her for that—Salazar was the worst kind of playboy and would've driven Mother Theresa to cheat on him. But Justin had thought Ceinlys would be more careful. She had a lot more to risk by cheating. The prenup she'd signed ensured she'd lose everything if she misbehaved.

"So…this woman just looked you up out of the blue?" he asked.

"Not exactly. She wants some money."

He sighed. He should've anticipated this and created a way to insulate her from greedy acquaintances and so on. People were going to know—already knew, in fact—that she was married to him, which to them was like winning a jackpot. Money brought out all the roaches. "I'm sorry. I hope you told her to contact my lawyer."

She snorted. "I don't know your lawyer. And I thought she was Dad's, so I wanted him to take care of her. She says her mother has cancer."

"Let me guess. She wants you to pay for some expensive chemotherapy. Or no, wait…some new kind of experimental drug. One that costs a lot because it's not in mass production yet."

She turned around. "That's pretty cynical."

A frown was pulling her eyebrows together, and he put his forefinger on the spot. "Because honey," he said gently, "that's always how it is. So what happened?"

"Dad told me she wasn't his kid because he'd never slept with anybody in Provo, the city where she's from. He also said"—her breath hitched—"I wasn't his."

"*What?*"

"He knew about Mom's affairs. He had a vasectomy after Shane was born. He said there was no way I could be his, but he looked the other way because he didn't mind 'another mouth to feed.'"

If Vanessa hadn't needed him right then, he would've driven back to the Pryce mansion and beaten the crap out of her father. Salazar Pryce had lost the right to judge and say cruel things the moment he'd decided to cheat on his wife. Everyone knew he hadn't even tried to be faithful. He'd started banging other women within a year of the marriage.

Vanessa's gaze lowered. "He told me to get out. But it explained so much about how he's treated me."

"Was he nasty to you?" Justin asked, mentally starting a list of Salazar's sins.

"It was more like he was always…preoccupied whenever I was around."

"Bastard."

"I thought maybe he was busy. I mean, he already had four rambunctious boys… Anyway, I think I was just in shock when Dad told me."

"Do you want me to take care of your sister?"

"What do you mean by 'take care of' her? Don't ignore her or send her away. She might be telling the truth."

"Even so, I don't like opportunistic parasites."

"She might be desperate to save her mom. I don't blame her."

Justin sighed. "Okay. Let me check her out. If she's who she says she is and her mother really has cancer, I can see about helping them. But if not, I'm going to make sure she never bothers you again." It wouldn't end at that. He would make sure she paid for causing Vanessa pain.

"Okay. Her cell phone number is in my purse. She wrote it on a napkin."

Justin nodded.

"And Justin?"

"Yeah?"

She reached out and took his hand, twining their fingers together. "I'm glad you're with me."

His heart swelled so fast and so unexpectedly, it was like his chest would burst. "So am I."

"I think I want to nap. Will you stay with me until I fall asleep?"

"Of course." He kissed their linked hands and watched as she went drowsy and then, eventually, slept.

How odd that things had gotten so much more complicated. He'd assumed that once she was his and their marriage had been made public, their lives would settle down into a simple rhythm and her worries would ease. Instead, circumstances were conspiring to pull her away from him emotionally.

For the first time, he had the thought that marriage and a baby might not be enough to keep her.

NINETEEN

OUT IN THE LIVING ROOM AGAIN, JUSTIN gave himself a few minutes to consider Vanessa's situation. He wanted to get started on this mysterious half-sister, but the whole thing had to be handled delicately.

Very delicately. Salazar apparently knew about Ceinlys's other men but had been decent enough not to use the information against her. However, if it came out publicly that she not only had other lovers but had passed off one of their children as her husband's, then the divorce would almost certainly become uglier. Justin didn't want that, as much to protect Vanessa as to protect Ceinlys herself.

He could use his family's usual investigator, but the man was a long-time friend of Barron's, and Justin didn't want his great-uncle knowing about any of this. It was none of his business.

He considered. *The Lloyds have an investigator who won't say anything to anyone…*

Justin called Kerri. "Hello, beautiful."

"Hello, handsome. What's up? I thought you'd be on a honeymoon."

"I'm taking a bathroom break."

"Eww. Are you calling me from a bathroom?"

He chuckled. "I'm actually at Vanessa's place right now. I was hoping you could call Pattington and give me a referral."

"What's the matter?"

"It's some delicate stuff that I don't want anybody knowing, especially Barron."

Kerri made a sympathetic noise. "I totally hear you on that. He can be so nosy."

"Tell me about it. So, Ms. Lloyd, how's pregnancy treating you?"

"Not too bad. I feel nauseous, and sometimes I get emotional, but other than that it's fine."

"You get emotional? Wow."

"It's the hormones," she groused. "The stupidest thing can set me off. It's, like, a thousand times worse than PMS."

"Poor Ethan."

"I know. Thankfully he loves me enough to put up with it."

"A man among men. All right, listen, just hook me up with Pattington, and I'll owe you."

"Give me about ten minutes. And here's his number." She rattled off the investigator's digits. "Good luck."

Justin waited exactly ten minutes and dialed Pattington's number. A man said, "Hello?"

"Justin Sterling."

"Kerri told me to expect your call. What's the problem?"

"Peggy from Provo." He looked down at the napkin he'd fished out of his wife's purse and read the numbers. "That's her cell. She's in L.A. right now. She claims to be my wife's half-sister. Apparently Ceinlys Pryce had an affair."

If Pattington was surprised, it didn't show in his tone. "And you want me to check her out with an eye toward…?"

"Nothing in particular. I just want to know about her for the moment. Get a reading."

"Anything else?"

Justin was about to say that would do, then he remembered how worried Vanessa had been about Shane's whereabouts. "Find out where Shane Pryce is. You can bill everything to me privately. Do *not* send anything to my office or my assistant."

"Is this your private cell phone?"

"Yes."

"Got it."

WHEN VANESSA AWOKE, SHE WAS ALONE IN THE bedroom. She lay there, staring at the ceiling. Her eyes felt gritty and painful, her throat numb and achy—fallout from her conversation with Salazar. Thank god Justin had been around to listen and help her deal with it.

Her stomach growled, and she finally got up. She'd lost her breakfast, and hadn't eaten anything since. Despite occasional morning sickness, her appetite seemed to be stronger than ever, and she was doing her best to eat food rich in nutrients.

In the kitchen, Justin slapped five huge slices of roast beef on whole-wheat bread and topped the whole thing with horseradish sauce and another piece of bread. "Hey. Feeling better?" he asked.

"A little." She went closer. "That looks good."

"Want some? I can make another."

"Mmm… Half would be about right."

He nodded and cut it diagonally. He put it with a pickle spear and pushed the plate her way. "Anything to drink?"

"OJ if we have any."

"We do." He served it out of the fridge. She glimpsed tons of food inside and tilted her head.

"Did you go shopping?"

"Yup."

"I didn't know you could find your way around a supermarket."

He gave her a strange look. “Where do you think I get my food? Mars?”

“I thought, I don’t know, that you had people who did that kind of work for you.”

“Yes and no. I may not be a gourmet cook, but I can fend for myself.” He pulled out the ingredients for another sandwich. “And yes, I know how to buy groceries.”

She nodded and started nibbling on the sandwich. It was surprisingly good. “I wonder how I’m going to tell my brothers about Peggy…and what Dad said.”

Justin’s hands went still for a moment. “Do you want to tell them?”

“I don’t know. There’s a part of me that says they have the right to know, but I’m also afraid that it’s going to change our relationship.” She bit her lower lip. “Even if Mom had an affair, we’re still siblings through shared experience. I mean, they’re the only brothers I know.” Even Dane—infuriating and insensitive as he was—meant something to her.

“Yeah, I understand.”

She eyed him warily. “Do you want to tell your family?”

He waved her concern away. “It’s none of their business who your real dad is. All that should matter to them is that I chose you.”

But had he? He always seemed to know exactly what to say to make her feel that honeyed warmth, but he was fudging the details of their marriage. There never had been any choice. It had been about her getting pregnant unexpectedly and him doing the right thing.

"You all right?" he asked.

"I'm fine," she said, forcing a smile. The timing didn't seem right to discuss the mess that had thrown them together. Maybe one day, when she didn't feel as though something was coming to take back what had been given to her, she would be able to talk to him more openly. "I think… I think I should tell my brothers what Dad said."

"Want me to be there with you?"

"Yes, that'd be great. And afterward we can decide what we can do about Peggy. I don't want to ignore her."

"Don't worry about that. I already took care of it."

"You did?"

"I'm going to check out her story first, make sure she's not trying to take advantage of you. Then if she's being honest, I'll give her some money to help with her mother's care."

"Thank you. I know you don't have to."

"If she's really your half-sister, she's family. And it's just money. It's not like we don't have enough of it."

She nodded, but she knew the truth. The money was Sterling money, not hers. She knew better than to rely on anyone. It'd been drilled into her since she'd been old enough to understand what her mother was saying—if she didn't earn it herself, it wasn't hers.

Before she lost her nerve, she texted her brothers about getting together to talk. She emphasized how important it was, to ensure Dane would come. Her oldest brother had the annoying habit of avoiding family gatherings. She'd also let them know it was just them, no parents. That might encourage her oldest brother to show up.

"Do you mind entertaining yourself for a bit while I go over to Mom's?" Vanessa said. She needed to talk to Ceinlys.

Justin gave her his rental keys. "Take this."

"Thanks." She kissed him. "I'll try not to ask you to come pick me up this time."

"No, you should call me if there's any problem. That's what being married means—taking care of each other."

She nodded with a small smile. It was sweet that her husband believed it, but experience had taught her that marriage had nothing to do with taking care of each other.

VANESSA SLOWED DOWN OUTSIDE HER MOTHER'S condo, looking for a parking spot. She found one not too far from her mother's Mercedes and sighed with relief. *Don't know why I didn't call first*. Ceinlys was busy, with a calendar full of social obligations.

Her mother buzzed her in, and soon Vanessa was standing in the living room.

"If I'd known you were coming, I might have bought some orange juice. Nothing else calmed my stomach," Ceinlys said. She was dressed casually in a slim black and white cotton dress that went down to mid-shin. "I only have water, milk…a little wine."

"Water's fine. Sorry to drop in like this, but it's important," Vanessa said, sitting down.

Ceinlys brought out a glass. "What could be more important than your secret marriage?"

Vanessa's face grew warm at the reminder of her elopement. In a way, she could see how her mother might be just a teeny bit peeved about not being able to have a grand wedding for her only daughter. On the other hand, would her father have been okay with it? She wasn't even his. "Why didn't you tell me I wasn't Dad's?"

The smile on her mother's face didn't change, but her eyes shuttered. "What are you talking about?" she asked, her diction a tad too precise.

"Dad had a vasectomy after Shane was born."

A small spot on her mother's cheekbone twitched. "You must be mistaken. Of course he did nothing of the sort."

"There's no mistake. My step-sister came to see me."

"Your step-sister? Vane—"

"Peggy Teeter. From Provo."

"Oh, her." Ceinlys's mouth set in a stubborn line. Vanessa knew that look. Her mother wasn't even going to entertain the idea. "The woman is an extortionist. She approached me first, asking for money. When I told her no, she said I owed her and that she'd get what she was due no matter what it took. If she approaches you again, call the police."

Vanessa shook her head. "I thought she was another one of Dad's, so I went over to confront him."

"Well, you shouldn't have."

"Why not? It was important to me. That's when he told me I wasn't his daughter."

Ceinlys closed her eyes. "I told that boy *never* to mention my name."

"Who was he? What was he like?"

"A poet I met at a party. He was dashing and interesting, and unlike Salazar, he had no money or prospects. But he made me feel like I was the most precious thing in the world. Which is probably why I fell for him that night." Ceinlys shook her head. "And it was only the one time. I told him it was over and never to approach me again. He was upset, but he accepted my decision. That's the convenient thing about those wounded artist types. They think nobody understands them and the whole world is against them." She shook her head. "It was quite easy to persuade him I was a mercenary harlot who was too interested in money to be with him."

Vanessa flinched, hating the way her mother talked about herself. That was the same horrible stuff that some jerks whispered behind her back—Ceinlys Pryce loved Salazar's money too much to divorce him. But given how much her mother doted on her children, Vanessa suspected it was losing custody that had kept her with her husband in the early years. "What was his name?"

"He called himself Klein."

"Is that his real name?"

"I have no idea. Never particularly bothered to find out. It wasn't important."

Vanessa bit her inner cheek. What little patience she had was seeping away, but it would be pointless to take it out on her mom. "Did you tell him about me?"

"No. I didn't want to give him an excuse to cling. He couldn't have been with me in any case. It simply wouldn't have worked."

"But the daughter he had with another woman seems to have found me somehow."

"You don't know if she's telling the truth. She might be conning all of us. I'd ignore her if I were you. Or, if she proves persistent, obtain a restraining order. It wouldn't be difficult."

"I plan to check her out before I do anything," Vanessa said. Then unable to help herself, she asked, "Did you love him?"

Ceinlys shook her head. "I enjoyed the way he made me feel, but I never loved him. By then I knew too much about how relationships worked to give in to a silly fantasy."

Vanessa thought back to Justin, how he made her feel safe and cared for, and how that turned her insides gooey and warm. "How do you separate the two?"

"Quite easily. I remind myself of the one time when I didn't, and how it hurt me."

"If you regret marrying Dad, why didn't you divorce him earlier? Even if you didn't get anything in the settlement, you would've been able to start over with another man. One who might have loved you and given you children."

Ceinlys's eyes were sad even as she smiled. "Once was enough, dear. I couldn't do it again." She folded her slim hands together. "Are you going to tell your brothers?"

"Yes. They should know."

"I see. Well, that probably is the right thing to do." Ceinlys uncrossed her legs and placed both feet flat on the floor. "Is there anything else you want to know?"

"Yes. How is everything going for you?"

Ceinlys's smile was genuine this time. "Oh, marvelously. I've never been better."

TWENTY

After a brief internal debate, Vanessa decided to have the meeting at her place. Mark offered one of his restaurants, but that was too public. She bought some pre-made finger foods and hors d'oeuvres from the local organic grocery store and laid everything out. Her brothers could eat like horses, although she wasn't sure how much appetite they'd have once she dropped her bomb.

She rubbed clammy hands down her denim capris. Nerves fluttered in her belly, and jittery energy crackled along her skin.

Justin laid a gentle hand on her shoulder. "Hey, it's going to fine."

"Yeah," she said tightly, and forced a smile. "Of course."

They didn't have to wait very long. All her brothers—except Shane—showed up within five minutes of each other, entering her living room one after another. Jane and Hilary had also come, since they were more or less family now as well.

Vanessa had always thought of her place as large and comfortable, but with so many people inside she felt claustrophobic.

Breathe. You can do this.

"Thanks for coming, everyone," she said, rubbing her hands together.

"I don't know what's so important that we have to talk face-to-face," Dane said, his voice cool. "You could've just emailed us."

"This is…extremely personal," Vanessa said. "Why don't we sit down?"

"You mind if I grab something to eat first? I haven't had a bite since ten thirty," Mark said.

She shook her head, amazed her restaurant owning brother went hungry. "Yeah, fine. Let's get some food and sit down then. I think it's better I say it when you're seated."

Dane gave her an odd look. "What did you do?"

"Nothing," she muttered.

"Did you hear from Shane?" Iain asked.

"No. But I saw Ginger with some other guy."

A stunned silence filled the room. Then Dane erupted. "*What?*"

"Justin was there too."

"That bitch."

"I wouldn't be too quick to judge," Justin said dryly. "She said Shane dumped her."

"She's lying," Dane said. "That boy's been whupped since high school."

"Maybe he became un-whupped," Vanessa said. "Regardless, if he decided he no longer wants her and broke it off cleanly, it's all good. They'll be spared the expense and hassle of a wedding."

Dane's cold look said he still held Ginger in the wrong, but Vanessa ignored it. He'd think whatever he wanted, and the issue between Shane and Ginger wasn't something she wanted to talk about.

"So is that why you wanted to have us here?" Iain asked.

"Dane's sort of right about this one. You could've just texted us," Mark said.

"No. Ginger is actually kind of…minor news. Please sit down."

They did, including Jane and Hilary, who were looking at Vanessa with concern.

Vanessa stayed on her feet and clasped her hands together. "There's no easy way to say this, so… I met my half-sister recently."

Everyone except Justin and Dane froze. Dane sighed and said, "Do you suppose we can sue the condom company Dad used? This is getting ridiculous."

"Is this half-sister for real?" Iain asked.

Mark gulped down some water. "Does she want fifty million bucks too?"

"No. She's actually, um, not related to Salazar at all. Or...you."

"Huh? But if she's your half-sis—"

"She and I share a father. And it's not...Dad. Mom took a lover back in the day and she's his daughter." Vanessa looked around. "Just like I am."

Dane's expression twisted like he'd just eaten a bug. "Let me guess. Now that she found out you're a rich man's wife, she wants to share in the bounty."

She flinched. That was the first thing Dane was worried about? "It wasn't quite like that. She said her mother had cancer."

"What does that have to do with you?" Dane asked.

"She asked me to help pay for her mother's treatment."

Dane laughed. "Don't tell me you fell for that line. You're a lawyer!"

Vanessa scowled. "What does being a lawyer have to do with this?"

"Because I'm sure you've heard the sorts of lies people tell to get something for nothing. Haven't you dealt with cases that are essentially legal extortion? Everyone has a mother or child with cancer when they discover a rich relative."

She hated it when Dane was right, if for no

other reason than that it only made him more cynical. "I'm pretty sure she's not expecting me to wire her money right this minute."

Dane snorted.

"I'm having her investigated," Justin said. "So don't worry."

"Well, it's nice that somebody's thinking things through. No matter what, I still wouldn't give her a penny. If you do, you're going to be inundated with people giving you the same sob story," Dane said.

"I doubt that," Mark said.

Dane's lip curled. "Do you think Mom's only had one lover? If they think there's money to be had, they'll all come out of the woodwork with their hands open. Mark my words, Vanessa. You're going to draw a big fat target on your back if you're not careful."

"Fine. I'll take that into consideration." It was better to give in than to argue endlessly with Dane. He saw the bad in everyone.

There was a general silence that stretched. Finally, Vanessa couldn't take it any longer. "Is… that all any of you have to say?"

"Did you expect something else?" Dane asked.

Hilary spoke up. "I think she means the thing about how she's not Salazar's daughter."

"What's there to say?" Iain shrugged. "Did you think we might not consider you our sister because of that?"

"You're still our sister." Dane's tone was flat as though he was reciting an encyclopedia entry. "Same mother."

Mark rolled his eyes. "Could you *be* any less sensitive?" He turned to Vanessa. "You're our sister. Nothing's changed. The years we spent growing up together didn't vanish because you learned that you're not Dad's daughter." Suddenly, his eyes widened. "Is this why you wanted to talk here? You were worried about our reaction?"

Vanessa nodded. "I didn't take the news very well when I found out."

"Aw, jeez."

"It's pretty shocking news," Jane said. "But I don't think people are going to love you any less for who your father is. Or isn't. You had no control over that."

Tears sprang to Vanessa's eyes. Sniffling, she wiped them away impatiently. It was so silly for her to cry when there was nothing but relief in her heart. It had to be the pregnancy hormones.

"You shouldn't have stressed about it. It's bad for you and your baby," Hilary said. "Happy thoughts. Everything's going to be fine."

Vanessa nodded, praying Hilary was right.

HILARY AND JANE DECIDED TO STAY WITH VANESSA, so Justin asked Dane for a ride to the Pryce mansion to pick up her car. The butler hadn't returned it yet, and he didn't feel like waiting any longer.

As the Lamborghini made its way through the traffic at exactly the speed limit, Justin said, "Don't ever try to manipulate Vanessa again."

A beat, then Dane said, "What's this about?"

"Her drive to make partner."

Dane laughed, the sound dry. "And she wonders why lawyers have shitty reputations. Did she tell you what she was originally planning to do?"

Justin tilted his head.

"Child advocate. Rewriting happy endings for kids with fucked up family lives…like that would retroactively change her childhood. But going into that field wasn't going to work."

"Why not?"

"Grandmother would've staged a heart attack… and probably blamed Mom for it. Mom would've been mortified. Dad probably would've found another woman to bang so he could pretend everything was fine. And Vanessa would've realized soon enough nothing can change the past.

"She's better off working for the bloodsuckers. They don't give you false hope or pretend to be something that they're not. But now that she's your wife, I'll let you deal with her." Dane stopped the car in front of the mansion.

Justin climbed out, and Dane drove away. Was he right about her family's potential reaction? Given how close she was to her mother, the whole mess would've been devastating for her.

It was strange to think Dane had actually done her a favor by challenging her—in his own way—to make partner. He wasn't the nurturing, caring type.

Shaking his head, Justin looked at the mansion. It was brightly lit, illuminating a garden full of animal-shaped shrubs and a cheery water fountain. But what dark shadows lurked inside.

When Justin rang, it was a middle-aged housekeeper who answered. She was short, with a comfortably rounded face. A polite smile didn't do anything to alleviate her homeliness, something Ceinlys had undoubtedly taken into consideration. It was one thing for her husband to have mistresses in other cities, something else to have one under the same roof.

"I'm Justin Sterling." He gestured at Vanessa's Mercedes. "Here to pick it up."

"Oh, you're her husband." The housekeeper's smile gained warmth. "Is she all right? I heard glass breaking while she was in Mr. Pryce's library."

"What are you talking about?"

Lines deepened between her eyebrows. "I think he might have thrown something against the wall while yelling 'Get out.' An awful argument."

"Are you sure?" Salazar knew Vanessa was pregnant. How could he throw things at her?

"I cleaned up the broken glass."

Fury like an Arctic storm whipped through him. "Where is Salazar?"

"In his study. The second floor, fourth door to the right."

Justin took the winding stairs two at a time to the upper level, where the ceiling was as high as a cathedral's. The study had double doors, and he wrenched them open.

"Justin. What a surprise," Salazar said from his desk. His rolled up sleeves revealed ropey arm muscles underneath age-thinned skin. He smelled faintly of shower gel, and moisture glistened in his hair.

"Is it true you threw a glass at my wife?"

"Why don't you ask her?"

"She'll try to protect you, so she won't tell me the truth."

"Why would she do that? She's not even my child. Didn't she tell you?"

Tension tightened Justin's neck and shoulders. The nerve at the back of his head throbbed. He dragged in some air. "Even though you raised her as your daughter, thankfully she's not like you. But I'm different. Don't you ever raise your voice or use violence against my wife."

Salazar's eyebrow rose with an arrogance that could only have come from a lifetime of living impervious to harm. "Or what?"

"I'll ruin you."

"Ruin me? That's a good one. You're too much like Vanessa, always too soft-hearted for her own good. That's why she married you, isn't it?"

Justin gave him a cold smile. "I'm Barron Sterling's heir. Not even her pleas would change my mind should I decide to destroy you. Surely you've heard why Barron's wife never tried to know what he was up to."

Everyone knew the story. Ethel Sterling hadn't wanted to get involved in her husband's dealings because her interference or suggestion for leniency would only egg him on to be harsher than he'd intended.

Justin continued, "Vanessa is my wife, not to mention pregnant with my child. You'll show her the respect she deserves. Do you understand?"

Salazar glared at him, and Justin glared right back. Finally the older man sat back and waved negligently. "Fine."

Justin breathed in with satisfaction and left the house in Vanessa's car. Underneath the leather was the scent of her. It was good that he'd come and found out about Salazar's unacceptable behavior toward Vanessa. But she should've told Justin from the beginning. He didn't want to worry that she was hiding things from him, especially if they were things that hurt her. His parents had always been open with each other, and he had a sinking feeling that without that, their marriage was a house built on a crumbling foundation.

TWENTY-ONE

SINCE VANESSA WAS FORCED INTO A LONG vacation, she decided she and Justin should go out of town. It wasn't often she was given two weeks off—in fact, she couldn't think of the last time—and she didn't want to stay in town and risk running into Peggy again.

She didn't seem dangerous, but now that Vanessa was calmer, she realized Justin and Dane had valid concerns about the woman's true motives. Besides, the way Peggy had revealed herself only when she thought she could get something and the way she'd made the first contact under false pretense weighed on Vanessa's mind. There was probably some desperate anxiety on Peggy's part, but at the same time, Vanessa would've preferred honesty from the very beginning. Now she felt like she couldn't trust Peggy entirely. She was like a witness behaving badly—withholding information here and there, only divulging more when she had no choice. Witnesses like that often changed their stories as well.

"You know, we should visit your mother," Vanessa said in the dark, her voice low and mellow. Justin had taken her so tenderly earlier, and her body was still quivering from the liquid pleasure that lingered. She pressed her back closer to him. She liked the way he enveloped her at night entirely too much, but she couldn't pull away. "I'm sure she's heard about our wedding and wants to see us face-to-face." She'd met Blanche Sterling socially years ago, but didn't really know much about Justin's mother.

"She called me a few days ago. She wants to see you too."

"Are you up for a trip? I don't know what your schedule is like."

"My schedule's flexible. We can go whenever you feel like."

Vanessa frowned as a thought occurred to her. "Do you think she'd rather fly out to see us?"

"No. She doesn't travel anymore."

"Why not? I remember how she used to travel a lot with your father."

"After he passed away, she sort of became a hermit. She doesn't even travel for family Thanksgivings."

"I'm sorry. That's kind of tough. Where does she live now?"

"Harrisburg. It's a small town in Ohio. But Nate and I visit her after the festivities. She really doesn't mind being alone. I think she enjoys the solitude."

Vanessa turned around to look at Justin. In the dark, she could barely make out the sharp, clean lines of his face. It was amazing how he was hers. She felt like this was a dream and she'd wake up alone without him or the baby.

What kind of a mother would she make?

Her only role models were her own mother and grandmother. Ceinlys loved her children—of this Vanessa had no doubt—but she didn't always express that affection very well. And she always seemed distracted and discontent, even though she faked happiness well when she knew people were watching. Nobody would've known how miserable Ceinlys was by looking at her. And she'd relegated almost every aspect of taking care of Vanessa to the nannies.

Then there was Shirley Pryce. Nobody was meaner or more cutting under the genteel exterior. She'd always made it clear that she considered Ceinlys to be beneath Salazar. Contemptible even.

She had also repeatedly told Vanessa a girl should never try to be too smart, too educated or too outspoken. A woman should strive not to embarrass her man, that was all.

"I don't blame you for making that mistake," her grandmother would say. "It's not your fault.

How can you know any better with a mother like Ceinlys?"

And unlike her brothers, Vanessa was the child who often did wrong according to her grandmother. Had Shirley, old but still very sharp, suspected Vanessa might not be Salazar's?

"What are you thinking?" Justin asked.

"Nothing." Vanessa wrapped her arms around him, not wanting to spoil their time in the dark by talking about her family. "Nothing at all."

Blanche's place in Harrisburg was a cozy cottage on a five-acre lot, a small section of which was a vegetable and herb garden. The house exterior was made of rough, earth-tone rocks, and the bright sun beat down on a red roof. A couple of apple trees grew in front, and a few long-eared rabbits hopped away as Justin's car pulled up.

Vanessa took in the house. It wasn't anything like what she'd pictured. She'd assumed Blanche would live in a mansion almost as grand as Barron's in Houston. She could certainly afford one. But Harrisburg wasn't even conveniently located. Vanessa and Justin had driven their rental for two hours after landing along lonely, deserted roads, some of which apparently didn't even have names.

"Why here?" Vanessa asked. "She could live anywhere she wants."

"To make sure it won't be easy for Barron to bug her or summon her." Justin put a hand on the small of her back. "Just a little rebellion against him for taking me from her."

"What do you mean?"

"She wanted to keep me at home, but Barron wanted me with him, so he could 'groom' me."

"Not many women would object to their son inheriting twenty-five billion dollars."

"Mom's not cut from the usual cloth." Justin's hand tightened behind her. "Watch your step."

"I'm fine." The path leading to the house was made of smooth pebbles, but Vanessa was an expert stiletto walker.

The aroma of bubbling soup and fresh biscuits hit her the moment Justin opened the heavy wooden door, and she had to smile at her own preconceptions. She'd assumed the place would be like her family's mansion with its cool, wax- and cleanser-scented air.

The interior was all warm earth-tone tiles and rugs and old wood with off-white stucco walls. A painting in the living room featured a view of the ocean; a sunset spilled orange over the water and palm trees swayed in the breeze. It somehow didn't quite seem to go with the rest of the place.

Justin noticed her gaze. "That's the place where she met my dad," he said. "She was working at a resort there."

Blanche came out of the open kitchen, her sneakers quiet. Stove heat had turned her cheeks rosy. Her hair spread out around her face like a fluffy silver cloud. She wasn't wearing a single piece of jewelry, but her dark eyes sparkled. She wore a pink long-sleeve shirt and blue jeans, all simple cotton. The white and green apron on her read *Home, Sweet Home* in a fire-truck red.

"Welcome!" she said, extending her arms.

"Mom!" Justin gave her a tight hug, his large frame enfolding Blanche's much smaller one.

Vanessa stood behind him, her hands clasped. Justin had put on a casual shirt and khakis, but she'd chosen a discreet black designer dress, a brand new pair of stilettos and the pink pearls Ceinlys had given her when she'd graduated from Stanford Law. Suddenly she felt overdressed and ridiculous—despite being in a favorite outfit that had never failed to boost her confidence. Still, she pasted on a polite smile.

"Introduce me to your wife," Blanche said, finally pulling away after a moment.

"Mom, Vanessa. Vanessa, Mom."

"How do you do?" Vanessa said in her smoothest debutante voice. Thank god her grandmother had insisted on her completing an etiquette course. At that time she'd thought it was the silliest thing ever, but now she clung to every lesson.

"No need to be so formal, my dear." Blanche clasped Vanessa's hands. "That's what Barron expects, not me. I'm just family." She gestured at the dining table. "Please, sit. I know it was a long drive from the airport. Do you want some soup? Or if you prefer, I have whole wheat bread and biscuits with organic butter."

"Soup and bread sounds lovely." Vanessa sat at the table.

"What about lamb?" Justin asked, taking a seat next to her

"That's for dinner, silly boy."

Blanche served everyone. The soup was homey, with a light broth, had delicious vegetables and beans, and was topped with shredded cheese.

"It's too bad you have to leave tomorrow," Blanche said.

"Work. What can I say?" Justin popped half a biscuit into his mouth. "Barron's basically retired, even though he won't formally announce it."

"That's so like him. Thank heavens he doesn't bother me with family events anymore."

"He can't make you travel."

"Especially since I don't care about his money." Blanche turned to Vanessa. "Justin can tell you, I value my privacy now. Too old to be gallivanting around. I heard you're pregnant. If anything's not to your liking, I can always get you something else."

"That won't be necessary. This is perfect."

"I'm so glad you're here, Vanessa." Blanche beamed. "Never thought Justin would marry, what with him unable to date any girl for long."

Vanessa forced a smile, then busied herself with eating. If Blanche only knew about their dating history, she wouldn't be as kind. She'd believe Vanessa had used her son, stringing him along. Having grown up watching her grandmother, she knew how things were perceived, especially by mothers-in-law.

But at the same time she couldn't help but wonder if Blanche would be different from Shirley Pryce, who would have died rather than be seen in a kitchen…or wearing an apron.

As the day went on, it became obvious that Justin adored his mother. While Vanessa rested on the living room sofa—having been practically ordered to do so—he went to the kitchen to help Blanche with cooking and clean-up. They laughed often, their voices light.

Blanche must be a great mother. All Vanessa's brothers—except possibly Dane—loved Ceinlys, but their interactions with her were always subdued, with a hint of strain. If they laughed once, it was a good time. Twice? Well, bring out the champagne.

The only child-rearing method Vanessa knew was handing kids off to nannies. Given how affectionately Blanche had treated Justin in just the few hours they'd been together that afternoon, Vanessa doubted that would be acceptable.

It was unfortunate there was no bachelor's degree in child rearing. Vanessa had hoped she could bumble along and figure things out without anybody judging her. But she'd thought wrong. Justin's mother was the standard by which he would judge her. And Vanessa didn't think she was going to measure up.

"I LIKE HER," BLANCHE ANNOUNCED, WHILE SHE watched Justin scrub the pan she'd used for the lamb chops. "She's smart...quiet, too. Thought she'd be more vivacious."

Justin looked at her. "Why?"

"Never known an attorney who didn't like to talk" She mused while munching on a stick of celery. "Maybe it's the pregnancy. I know how tired I was when I was expecting. No wonder she went to bed early."

"Must be," Justin agreed, bending to his work.

The dinner had been great—his mother's lamb chops were fabulous as usual—but Vanessa hadn't said or eaten much. Thankfully he was able to fill the silence with stories about their acquaintances and friends and family. Maybe Vanessa was just nervous. Understandable—if his experience with family dinners had been anything like hers, he would've been nervous too. And then there was the unfinished business with Peggy. It had to be weighing on Vanessa's mind, especially after Salazar's bombshell announcement. Fortunately, she was taking another nap on the living room couch.

He rinsed the pan and dried it. Blanche was old and frail now, but she didn't want to have a housekeeper around even though he'd offered to pay for one.

"So tell me about Ceinlys," Blanche said, starting the coffee machine. It gurgled. "I didn't want to ask right in front of Vanessa, but is she really divorcing Salazar?"

"Yes. It's true."

"My land. I can't believe it. They were meant to be together forever, even with all those mistresses of his."

"Everyone thought that."

"What changed?"

He shrugged. "I have no idea. Iain might know, but he didn't say."

"Well, no need to probe. I just hope it's not too stressful for the kids, especially your lady out there. Stress is terrible for pregnant women. I'm sure I don't have to tell you this, but be extra gentle with her. Pregnancy hormones are brutal." Blanche frowned. "I hope she can take some decent time off work. Lawyers work too much."

"Don't worry. She's on a special case at the firm."

"Really?" Blanche cocked her head, and Justin cursed inwardly. He never had been able to put anything past his mother. "Would that have anything to do with you?"

"Well." Justin cleared his throat. "It might."

"Justin. Does she know?"

"No, and she doesn't need to. It's not like it's going to affect her career there. This was during the time she wanted to keep our relationship quiet and secretive."

"Weren't you already married at that point?"

"Yes, but it didn't matter. She didn't want anyone to know we were a couple."

"How very odd," Blanche spoke slowly. "Did she tell you why?"

"Something about wanting a partnership on her own merit, not based on who she's married to."

"Do you believe that?"

"Why wouldn't I?"

"Your Aunt Annabella is a lawyer, and it took her thirteen years to make partner, and you know how smart she is."

Justin nodded. Not just smart, Annabella had graduated from Yale Law with honors.

"Vanessa's a bit too young—she's been with the firm for, what, about ten years?"

"Yeah."

"The chances of her getting a partnership are very slim, and soon everyone will know she's pregnant anyway." Blanche tapped neatly trimmed nails on the Formica counter. "I'm sure there's another reason."

A frown tightened his forehead. He'd wondered, but he'd chosen to accept Vanessa's decision at face value. But his mother was right. "Why would a woman want to keep something like that a secret?"

Blanche poured herself a cup of strong coffee, black, no sugar. Shc didn't offer any to Justin; he never drank it late in the evening. "Maybe to surprise somebody? Or maybe because you don't expect it to last? I didn't tell my parents about your father until he actually proposed. I couldn't believe he'd want to marry a girl from a lower middle class family when he could have had any woman he wanted."

"But we're marr—" Even as the words left his lips, it hit him. In Vanessa's experience, marriage didn't mean commitment and respect and love. It was a peculiar sort of trap that forced two people to stay with each other when they might be happier apart.

But she can't possibly think our future will resemble her parents'. He'd never done anything to make her believe he'd be like Salazar.

Blanche put a hand on Justin's sleeve. "Sometimes a woman needs reassurance. Maybe you should tell her how you feel."

"How did you know?"

"Oh, a mother's intuition. You're too proud, and as much as you want to believe you're not like Barron, you are very much like him from time to time. You're waiting for her to tell you first, aren't you?" Blanche took a slow sip of her coffee, her eyes on his. "A successful relationship is not like a business negotiation. Sometimes you have to make the first move, show your cards."

Justin nodded, more than a little perturbed by her observation. Was he really treating the marriage like a business arrangement? And more importantly, did Vanessa really expect it to fall apart? Justin was a firm believer in the power of both positive and negative thinking, of self-fulfilling prophecies, and it took more than one person to make a marriage work.

TWENTY-TWO

IT DEFINITELY TOOK MORE THAN ONE TO MAKE a marriage work.

Justin feigned an interest in the latest financial reports from Sterling & Wilson as they flew back to L.A. the next day, but he knew something was wrong. Vanessa had been asleep by the time he'd returned to their bedroom the night before, and since then she'd been aloof, maintaining a physical distance from him.

Now she was sitting across from him, eyes closed, arms crossed and chin down. But given the tension in her posture, he knew she wasn't sleeping.

At first he'd assumed she was just tired from the trip…and of course the pregnancy. She could be moody from time and time, and it wasn't a big deal. But she was shutting him out, and that he didn't care for.

"Let's have it. What are you upset about?" he asked.

She didn't open her eyes. "Not upset. Trying to sleep."

"You slept for over ten hours last night."

"Pregnant women sleep a lot."

"Not you. You never slept much anyway."

She sighed and cracked one eye open. "Pregnancy changes you. Besides, it's not like I have tons of work to do, so it's better I figure out something else to occupy my time." Her tone held an edge.

"If you're bored, maybe you can do some volunteering. Pro bono work or..."

"Can't take on anything like that. You never know when Highsmith will decide he needs me for something. And who knows? My current client might just get sued and actually need some genuine, honest-to-god legal help." She got up. "I think I'm going to lie down. I have a headache."

Justin watched her slip into the stateroom and reined in his temper. It would be ridiculous for him to confront her right now. Besides she might really not be feeling well. She was paler than usual, her manner subdued.

He checked his email and raised an eyebrow when he saw one from Pattington. The man had come through with information about Peggy Teeter.

Everything checks out. She has a mother in a cancer center. Lung cancer—bad, but treatable. Her father was a poet, and he lived in L.A. for two years when he was in his thirties. Details in the report (attached).

Justin scanned the report Pattington had sent. So Peggy really was Vanessa's half-sister.

Glancing at the closed door to the bedroom, he dialed Peggy's number.

"Hello?" came a tentative voice.

"Peggy Teeter?"

"Yes..."

"This is Justin Sterling, Vanessa Pryce's husband. I want to arrange to have your mother's cancer treatment taken care of."

"Oh. Hi. I…didn't realize she'd involve you."

Justin frowned. What had she thought Vanessa would do? Take care of the matter on her own? He was her husband. "Can you send the details to my assistant?" He gave her the email address.

"Of course." There was a pause. "Would you mind if we meet in person?"

Justin considered. "I have some time this afternoon, but it'll have to be quick."

"Sure. Do you mind if I pick the time and place? I'm returning to Provo to check up on my mother later today."

"That's fine."

"Can I text you at this number?"

"Use this one." Justin rattled off the public mobile number that he used with his executives and workers. "I'll bring Vanessa as well."

"No, please don't. Thanks, Justin." She hung up.

AS SOON AS THEY ARRIVED BACK AT THE CONDO, Vanessa changed into a casual dress and went out again. She didn't think she could talk to Justin without losing control. The conversation between him and his mother echoed in her head. She'd overheard it from the living room; when he had emerged from the kitchen she'd pretended to be asleep instead of confronting him in his mother's home. And now the things he'd said were simmering in her mind like a witches' brew.

She spotted Felix the moment she entered the Starbucks near the office. She waved at him while standing in line to get a decaf latte, then went over to his table.

"What's up? Hope it's not an emergency," he said. "I was surprised to get your call."

"It's not. You look good." And he did, sitting there in his conservative, perfect-for-the-office suit. Bitterness spread in her heart. Unlike her, he had a career of his own, without anybody meddling in it.

"Can't believe you're still in town. I thought you'd be in Acapulco or somewhere by now."

She forced a laugh. "Just because I have two weeks off doesn't mean Justin does." She leaned forward. "Hey, I know you're busy, but I need to talk to you about something you said."

He frowned. "Okay."

"You remember how you said how that silly forty-hour work I was doing was more important than it looked?"

"Yeah…"

"What made you say that?"

He shrugged. "I heard rumors that the work had something to do with Sterling & Wilson. A couple of the secretaries were talking about it."

The latte sat like poison in her belly. "The secretaries know too?"

"Well, it's just a rumor. But yeah, they're plugged in. All the work they do for the partners."

She pinched the bridge of her nose. "I can't believe this." Her cheeks flushed as humiliation mixed with anger.

"Why are you so upset?"

"Do you know why I wanted to keep my marriage to Justin quiet?" She didn't wait for a response. "I didn't want it to affect my career at the firm. Justin knew that too, but he hired Highsmith, Dickson and Associates anyway, and I'm sure the partners figured out there was something between us." Highsmith hadn't become head of the firm by being slow. "When I'm offered a partnership, I want it to be because I'm good at what I do, not because I'm married to Justin Sterling!"

"People knowing who your husband is doesn't make you a bad lawyer all of a sudden."

"No, but the—"

"Vanessa, hey. Calm down. Nobody makes partner in only ten years these days. And if you do, it'll be because the firm expects you to pull in enough business to justify that decision."

"It's just business? That's what you're saying?"

"Well, yeah. It's okay to use family connections for that. People hire people they like."

She choked back a hysterical laugh. She couldn't even use her family name anymore because she wasn't a real Pryce. Salazar wouldn't hire her firm, no matter what, and now it became clear why he'd warned her about that before.

Felix was giving her a shrewd look. "Are you sure there isn't another reason why you're upset about people knowing about your marriage?"

"What do you mean?"

"Why do people keep their relationships secret? Like us, when we were dating."

"It would've been awkward if people knew, especially since we were dating casually. It wasn't serious."

"Exactly." Felix smiled, a tinge of nostalgia in the curve of his lips. "We didn't want everyone to know when our relationship ended. So what about your marriage? It's not like getting hitched to somebody like Justin Sterling is a badge of shame. My guess is you didn't want anybody to know in case you went your separate ways."

"You do the pop psychology thing as a sideline?"

"You don't believe me?"

"Felix, there's no way our divorce would stay quiet."

"If you can marry somebody like him in secret, you can divorce him the same way." Felix finished his cappuccino. "And mock me all you like, but the fact is, everyone wants to keep their failures hidden from the world. You're a smart woman, Vanessa. Be honest with yourself."

Vanessa reached for her latte and held it like a shield. Honesty scared her; it usually told her something she'd rather not know. Sometimes illusions were better for one's peace of mind.

Except now it was too late.

TWENTY-THREE

After Vanessa walked out, Justin spent a few fruitless minutes trying to figure out what was bugging her, then gave it up as hopeless. Instead, he got in his car and drove to a downtown hotel lobby.

He checked his watch as he walked in. *Right on time.* A woman who matched the photo Pattington had sent was seated in a plush leather armchair that seemed to swallow her slim frame.

She wasn't gorgeous the way Vanessa was. If it hadn't been for Ceinlys's admission, he would never have guessed that this woman was related to his wife. Peggy had shaggy brown hair, styled with care and wax. Her features were even and pretty, but not exceptional enough to stand out. Still, she seemed to fit in with the luxury marbled surroundings somehow.

She got up when she noticed him. “Thank you so much,” she said. “I know you’re a busy man. And sorry about the venue, but I wanted to make it quick before I have to get back to my mother.”

“I thought you were living with a boyfriend.”

“Wow. You were thorough, weren’t you? We broke up yesterday, and I moved out.”

They sat down, taking two chairs near a hotel phone.

“So. What is this meeting about?” he asked.

“I just wanted to say thanks. And I’m curious about the man my half-sister married.”

“There are more than a few profiles and articles about me.” He kept his voice matter-of-fact. The first thing he’d learned was that people rarely wanted to see him just for shits and giggles.

“All carefully edited to help you maintain an image. I know how the media game is played.” Her gaze roamed his clothes, shoes, watch, haircut, giving him the uncomfortable but familiar sensation of being catalogued for assets. “It’s amazing, isn’t it? That she and I are related?”

“You can always take a paternity test if you’re so astounded,” he said somewhat unkindly. She could try all she wanted, but he wasn’t giving her anything more. If it hadn’t been for her cancer patient mom, she would’ve gotten nothing.

“That won’t be necessary,” Peggy said finally with a smile that felt oddly empty.

Enough of this. "Have you contacted my assistant?"

"Yes. She said everything's been taken care of."

"Then it looks like our business is concluded." He stood up.

"I'll walk with you. I'm leaving too anyway."

They went out together. In front of the main door, she turned to him. "This means the world to me. You didn't have to help."

"It's been my pleasure."

Placing a hand on his cheek, she rose on her toes and kissed him. "Thank you and good-bye. You know, when I first came to L.A. to try and get help from Ceinlys, and then Vanessa, I thought it was sort of unfair. They have this great life, and my mom's sick with cancer. But I see that maybe that's not the case. Vanessa's good fortune became mine."

Not much to say to that. He rubbed the back of his neck as it tingled suddenly.

Peggy laughed, breaking eye contact. "If you're ever in Utah, look me up. Bring Vanessa too if you like." Then she climbed into a waiting taxi.

EASING UP ON THE GAS, VANESSA BLINKED, THEN stole another glance in the rearview mirror. The man was definitely Justin, the woman now gone in the taxi.

Why was he meeting Peggy alone at a hotel? And unless Vanessa was mistaken, Peggy had kissed him.

The car behind honked, and Vanessa accelerated. Justin hadn't said anything about going out or meeting Peggy. He'd said he was having her investigated, but if everything had checked out, he should've told Vanessa…shouldn't he?

An old image of her father coming out of a hotel with one of his many mistresses flashed in her mind. The blonde had kissed her father's cheek chastely, like somehow the gesture would hide the fact that they'd been in a room, screwing each other's brains out. Vanessa had been too young to understand, but she supposed everyone else had… and had pitied her as a result.

Suddenly the dam she'd used to contain her doubts burst, and she started shaking. There were so many things that had gone wrong. By now, her firm probably fully expected her to bring the Sterling & Wilson business. And everyone knew about her marriage to Justin, so anyone who'd seen him with Peggy just now would probably start talking about her now the way they had her mother. And the baby…

She put a hand on her belly. Would it have the same kind of awkward and emotionally lonely childhood she'd had? Would she wind up like her mother, having more and more children, first to ensure her husband didn't stray, then to fill the enormous hole left by his inattention?

Maybe she should've never told Justin about the baby. Then none of this would've happened.

Tears filled her eyes, and she wiped them away impatiently. This wasn't like her. She didn't cry like a little girl at the prospect of trouble. She'd find a way around it or over it...or through it if she had to.

Nothing more, nothing less.

Stopping at a red light, she put on a headset and dialed Justin.

"Hey, Vanessa," he said, his voice washing over her like warm caramel.

"Where are you?" she asked.

"On my way home." He paused. "Are you downtown? If so, we can eat out."

She tried to think of a way to approach the matter delicately, but couldn't. "Did you have the firm put me on a restricted work schedule?"

There was a short pause. "Vanessa, it's not like that."

"Okay. Did you get an update on Peggy?"

"Yes. She checked out. So I'm going to pay for her mother's cancer treatment. It's not that much money anyway."

And how did she thank you? Vanessa swallowed the question. "That's generous of you. Even more generous to see her in person to do it."

Another pause. "She wanted to thank me in person, that's all."

"Mmm. And you had to meet at a hotel to do that?"

"Are you accusing me of something?"

"I'm not accusing you of anything. Just wondering."

"Vanessa, nothing happened." When she didn't say anything, he added, "Don't you trust me?"

"It's hard to trust you when you did something behind my back and didn't tell me. Like an idiot, I even complained to you about my work."

"I didn't know how you'd take it."

"So if you don't know how I'll take something, you can lie about it? Tell me this then: How do you think I'd take it if you told me you cheated on me?"

He cursed. "I'm not going to pay for your father's sins. Do you understand? I'm not him. The fact that you're even thinking that I'd break my vow to you is an insult to my character. You're being insecure and unreasonable."

Blood rushed through her, roaring in her ears. She could barely hear what he was saying. "I'm neither insecure nor unreasonable. Don't try to make it sound like I'm just being a hormonal woman."

"You are. You're always looking for reasons not to fully commit to anything because you're afraid. Guess what? I'm tired of your waffling. When you walked out on me in February, I put myself on a detox program to forget you because it's not possible to be with a woman like that."

Vanessa's jaw locked. He meant a woman like *her*. The only reason why he'd ever wanted her was the baby.

The precious heir to the Sterling & Wilson fortune.

Justin continued, "How can I carry the relationship by myself when you won't open up? When you want to treat it like some shameful thing? I have to be in an airplane accident for you to—"

Suddenly she heard a loud, continuous honk to her left. Her head swiveled. A huge black SUV was coming toward her. It was slowing down, but it wouldn't be quick enough.

Panic surged in her veins. Blood roared, and she raised her arm like somehow she could block the steel doom.

The impact of metal slamming into metal shook her like a rag doll. Glass shattered. Her arm snapped back and hit her in the face; her headset flew off her ear.

Pain seared through her. Then she drowned in black.

EVERYTHING WAS HAZY, DROWNED IN BLINDING light. There was the scent of disinfectants and bodies. People were shouting. Their voices sounded professional, authoritative.

Vanessa wanted to close her eyes again, but she couldn't. She wanted Justin with her right then and there, but he might not come, not after she'd accused him of cheating on her with Peggy.

Why had she reacted that way? She'd seen how easy it would be to lose him when his plane crashed in San Francisco. But instead of cherishing every moment together, she'd lived in fear of losing him—if not to an accident, then to another woman. He'd been right to accuse her of being insecure and unreasonable. And he shouldn't have to pay for Salazar's mistakes.

The gurney rattled, vibrating under her. Her face throbbed, and her chest and stomach felt like they'd been punched repea—

Her stomach.

The baby!

A sour tang of panic filled her mouth and throat. She couldn't lose the baby. It hadn't even had a chance at life.

Tears wet her eyelashes. It had to be her fault she was losing the baby. Instead of being grateful for the miracle, she'd questioned it, fretted over it and wondered if she truly wanted the responsibility of motherhood. She felt like she was being punished for those doubts. Why did it have to come to this before she realized what she really wanted?

She raised her hand. "My baby…" The words were barely a whisper.

"It's all right. We got you. Just relax," a nurse said, her voice more efficient than soothing.

No, they didn't get anything. Vanessa couldn't relax. Fear surged in her heart even as her grip on consciousness faded, and she slipped back into the dark.

TWENTY-FOUR

JUSTIN BURIED HIS FACE IN HIS HANDS, WILLING it to be a bad dream. Vanessa's three brothers, the two fiancées and Ceinlys sat with him. Nobody said anything.

The hospital smelled too much of chlorine and alcohol. Underneath was a stench of despair. The nurses and doctors were brisk and efficient, but their workmanlike competence did nothing to soothe his shock or calm his panic.

He'd been frustrated with Vanessa, and having her accuse him of something he hadn't done had frayed his temper. But the possibility that his harsh words might've had something to do with the accident ate at him. If she'd been one hundred percent focused on driving, maybe she would've noticed the SUV sooner and done something to avoid it. The cops hadn't said much except that the driver had been texting and run a red light.

"She's going to be okay," Iain said.

"You didn't see her when they brought her in." Justin had only a glimpse of her bloodied and abused body. She looked half-dead.

"A lot of times it looks worse than it is," Iain said, "especially if there's blood. See it with fights all the time. But she'll probably be okay. This is a great hospital, and the doctors are excellent."

"Here, have some coffee," said Jane. "It might help."

He took it gratefully and sipped the strong dark brew. It didn't do much to warm his cold inside, but it was nice to hold onto something so he wouldn't tear out his hair. "She's pregnant, you know," he said.

"Did they say anything about the baby?" Ceinlys said, her voice thin. Her face was pinched and pale, and her lipstick had worn off, leaving her lips bare and grayish pink.

"No." Justin forced his hands to relax around the coffee cup. He'd give anything to keep her and their baby safe. But his mind whispered money wouldn't be able to solve this problem. It hadn't been a lack of money that had killed his father. Just a careless teenage driver who was too busy fooling with his new GPS to pay attention to what he was doing. The kid had survived, but Justin's father hadn't.

Justin rose, unable to sit still anymore while morbid possibilities swirled in his mind. This wasn't like him. He never obsessed about all the *what ifs*.

That was one of the biggest reasons why Barron had decided to groom him as his heir.

"Lemme know if you hear anything," Justin said. "I need to—"

Iain stood. "I'll go with you."

Justin nodded, and they walked along the linoleum-covered hall together, their shoes clicking. Another group of harried looking staff rushed past them, and Justin paused and stared at their disappearing backs. Were they going that way because Vanessa was getting worse?

"She should be okay," Iain said. "She's a fighter."

"She was bloody. Soaked in it." Justin realized his hands were shaking, and he clenched them.

"I'm telling you, that can be anything. Maybe she cut herself during the accident. She needs you to be strong."

"We were arguing when she got hit."

They resumed walking.

"Do you love her?" Iain asked quietly, then raised a hand. "No, don't tell me. But if the answer isn't a hundred percent yes, let her go. Don't end up like my parents. They have a fucked-up marriage, no other way to say it. Big waste of a couple of lives. They could've been happier if they hadn't stayed together for the kids." He blew out a breath. "Joint custody, right? What I'm saying is, you don't have to lose the child just because you aren't married to Vanessa."

"Your parents really did a number on you guys, didn't they?"

"They probably did what they thought was best. But it wasn't always comfortable. And yeah, I'm sure it had something to do with the way we are. Everyone's shaped by their parents."

Justin said nothing. He knew all about Iain's issues with his parents. All of the Pryce siblings had gone to extreme lengths to be a certain way. Mark had been a notorious playboy until he got engaged, Iain had been far too controlled, Shane had committed himself to a girl too soon only to drag his feet about the wedding and disappear, and Dane was an insensitive asshole. And Vanessa…she had married her career—like it was going to fill the void in her heart—and distanced herself from everything.

Just because she'd been raised in moneyed luxury didn't mean she had the same advantages he did. She hadn't had his stable family life and upbringing. He should have been more understanding. She was his wife.

And he loved her.

The awful things he'd said to her haunted him. His meeting Peggy like that had undoubtedly looked suspicious to Vanessa. He shook his head, angry at himself. *I should've told her about Pattington's report first, discussed what I was planning to do. Gotten her input, instead of being high-handed and expecting her to accept my decisions.* He'd thought their marriage was doomed because she wouldn't carry her weight, but it was his autocratic nature that was killing it.

VANESSA OPENED HER EYES. THE WALLS IN HER room were white…with scuff marks…and the air smelled of disinfectant underneath the heady scent of fresh flowers. Machines beeped and pinged, and the metal frame bed was…narrow.

She didn't hurt all over anymore. What kind of medicine had they used? What about her baby?

A nurse came in and smiled at her. "How are you feeling?"

"Not in pain." Vanessa licked her dry lips. She wanted to ask about Justin—had he come by? But instead she asked, "Is my baby okay?"

"Yes. Your baby's fine. You sprained your wrist, and there were quite a few minor cuts—nothing serious—plus a blow to the head that gave you a heck of a nose-bleed. Basically, you're banged up and you're going to have raccoon eyes for a week or so, but you're fine. We checked everything thoroughly."

"Thank you," Vanessa whispered. "What time is it now?"

"Ten thirty. Your brothers dragged your husband out to get him to eat something."

He was here! Vanessa sagged. *Even after I was so stupid.*

The nurse went on: "He didn't want to leave you alone. I'll let them know you're awake."

"No, let them finish eating first."

"All right. Are you hungry?"

She shook her head. "Just tired."

"If you need anything, all you have to do is press the button here." The nurse showed her the call button and left.

Vanessa relaxed against the pillow and swallowed. Her baby was all right. Justin was here. Everything was going to be okay. She could feel it.

She dozed for a while. Then the door opened, and Justin walked in. She almost wept, her heart fluttering with relief. Mark and Iain followed, along with Hilary and Jane. Even Dane came. And her mother was there too. The only noticeable absence was Salazar.

Justin settled next to Vanessa and held her hand. Fatigue lined his face, but his eyes were warm. "I thought the nurse was mistaken when she said you were awake."

She smiled, linking her fingers with her husband's. "Nope. Awake and totally fine now."

"Oh, thank god." Ceinlys burst into tears.

"Mom, you're going to cry now?" Mark said weakly, while Iain handed her a handkerchief.

Hilary and Jane turned to Vanessa. "We're just glad you're okay."

"You could look worse," Dane said, which Vanessa took as equivalent to her mother's reaction.

"I want to go home," Vanessa said. "Now. The nurse said I'm fine."

"Whatever you want, sweetheart," Justin said, kissing her forehead. "Whatever you want."

Justin was somehow able to get her discharged so fast that they were on their way home within forty minutes. He was quiet as he drove; she held his hand, wanting the reassurance of physical contact.

He helped her get out and walk from the car. She gasped when she finally noticed her reflection in the mirror-shiny elevator door. "I look like a boxer. A boxer who just lost."

Justin squeezed her hand. "No, you won. You survived. Besides, you still look gorgeous."

"You are *such* a liar."

She yelped when he swept her off her feet and carried her over the threshold. "Isn't it a bit too late for this?" she said with a laugh.

"It's never too late. Where do you want to go?" he asked, turning on the light.

"I want to sit on the couch. I'm tired of lying down."

"Okay, but only for a bit," he said. "You need to rest."

She nodded. "Okay. Half an hour then."

Her legs felt rubbery, and her knees had started aching. She'd probably banged them against something in the accident. She didn't remember much of it.

"Do you want anything?" he asked.

"OJ?"

He returned with a glass of juice and sat next to her, taking her free hand. "Hey, listen…I'm sorry."

She stopped in the middle of raising her drink. "For what?"

"The things I said. I shouldn't have. And I should've told you about Peggy's situation before I went to meet her."

Vanessa shook her head. "I'm sorry I lashed out at you too. You were right; I was trying to make you pay for my father's…indiscretions." She blinked back tears. "When they took me to the hospital, I was so scared I'd lose you and our baby both. I was sure you wouldn't want to be with me anymore."

"Vanessa. I've wanted you since forever. I'm not going to give up on you over an argument." He turned her hand over, running his thumb over the wedding band. He kissed her on the mouth gently, careful of her bruises. "I love you, Vanessa. I've loved you for years and I'll always love you, no matter what."

"I love you too, Justin. I don't know why it's taken me so long to figure that out." Then she shook her head. "Actually, I do know. I was too afraid to take a chance."

"Do you think we can start over? I know you're worried we're going to end up like your parents, but I believe we can be better than our parents. And our child will be greater than us."

This time she let the tears fall. "You say the sweetest things."

"How can I not?" He put the glass of juice on the side table and took her gently into his arms. "We have the sweetest future."

TWENTY-FIVE

THE SINGER'S VOICE SOARED AS SHE SANG "Cheek to Cheek." The orchestra provided a romantic accompaniment.

The ivory hall was full of great food, drink and fresh flowers. In the center was a champagne fountain surrounded by ten layers of plumerias in full bloom. Liveried servers milled around with silver trays, making sure no guest went without the proper libations. Even though everyone in Vanessa and Justin's social circles had wanted an invitation to the reception, she'd chosen to keep the event on the smaller side, with only the people who mattered most to them—their friends and family.

Vanessa had quit her job soon after the accident. Working ridiculous hours for clients chosen for their ability to pay the most money no longer appealed, even if it meant she'd never be a partner. Better to start doing something meaningful with her life. She'd told Justin about her non-profit and her wish to be actively involved in it. Without hundred-plus hour weeks, she would finally be able to give it the attention it deserved. He'd offered to fund it, but that had ended up being unnecessary. Not when Gavin Lloyd had been managing its assets. She'd heard that he had the Midas touch, but the amount of money currently in Just and Proper Help's coffers was almost beyond her ability to comprehend. And it was all hers to help those in need.

Vanessa and Justin swayed to the song. Others came onto the dance floor, and Barron showed off some surprisingly fancy steps with Stella Lloyd.

Vancssa was almost into her second trimester, but she didn't show much, not with the white empire-waist dress she was wearing.

"This is exactly how it should've been done from the very beginning," Vanessa whispered into Justin's ear as he expertly led her. "I should've never try to hide our marriage."

"You had your reasons." Justin grinned. "Only two things matter now.

"What?"

"One, our baby is doing well."

She had to agree with that. "And two?"

"That you're mine."

She couldn't help but smile. "I love you."

He took her hand and laid it over his heart. "I love you."

EPILOGUE

THE MAN STOOD OUT ON THE SAND, FEELING the gritty scrunch under his toes. The weather was getting hot now—too hot, really—but he didn't want to stay inside the beach house.

He couldn't remember his name, but somehow he knew the house's security code. It still astounded him that no one had tried to stop him from using the credit cards in the wallet he'd found in his pocket. They all bore a name he didn't recognize, but—somehow—they were his. And so was the U.S. passport; there had been no trouble using it to go through customs in several different countries.

In the last few months, he'd visited the places he'd found stamped in the passport, hoping that something would jog his memory. Nothing did, but then again he couldn't exactly walk around asking people for help. He apparently had a lot of money—it was obvious from the kind of clothes in his bag and the treatment he received at airports and hotels. If he admitted that he couldn't remember who he was, he'd become a target.

Five men walked toward the beach. He watched them, wondering who they were. They didn't look like locals. They were white, fit and had the hard look of professionals. There was a housekeeper who called him "mister," but otherwise nobody had come to the place in the time he'd been there. A cold frisson of warning tingled at the back of his neck.

"Shane Pryce?" one of the men said.

Maybe. "Who are you?"

"Dane sent us."

"Who's Dane?"

"Your brother. It's time you come home."

WHAT'S NEXT?

Coming up next is *The Billionaire's Forgotten Fiancée*, featuring Shane Pryce (May, 2015). If you want to know when it's out, sign up for my mailing list at http://www.nadialee.net.

ABOUT NADIA LEE

New York Times and *USA Today* bestselling author Nadia Lee writes sexy, emotional contemporary romance. Born with a love for excellent food, travel and adventure, she has lived in four different countries, kissed stingrays, been bitten by a shark, ridden an elephant and petted tigers.

Currently, she shares a condo overlooking a small river and sakura trees in Japan with her husband and son. When she's not writing, she can be found reading books by her favorite authors or planning another trip.

To learn more about Nadia and her projects, please visit www.nadialee.net. To receive updates about upcoming works from Nadia, please visit www.nadialee.net to subscribe to her new release alert.

Made in the USA
Columbia, SC
27 February 2020

88451224R00186